A gift from the sea...

Corwin became aware that he was gripping something in his right hand. He looked down. He was still holding the silvery, glittery thing he had found within the grip of the dead sea creature. Somehow he had held onto it throughout his ordeal.

Corwin held it up and examined it. It *was* a shell, but not like any he had ever seen before. It was spiraled, like a coiled horn—opalescent, glimmering with many colors beneath a silvery sheen. Corwin's right hand itched and he shifted the shell to his left hand. Corwin stared down at his palm. There was a fresh welt in the skin, a welt distinctly in the shape of a sun.

How on earth did that happen? Corwin wondered.

Suddenly he felt a sharp pain in his gut, and the world spun violently around him.

Enjoy all three books in the *Water* Trilogy:

Water
BOOK TWO

REUNION

KARA DALKEY

AVON BOOKS
An Imprint of HarperCollins*Publishers*

Produced by 17th Street Productions,
an Alloy, Inc. company
151 West 26th Street, New York, NY 10001

Library of Congress Catalog Card Number: 2001118042
ISBN 0-06-440809-4

First Avon edition, 2002

Visit us on the World Wide Web!
www.harperteen.com

Chapter One

The sky overhead was black as a raven's wing, but the stars were already fading, and the horizon glowed through the lifting fog with the promise of a late summer's morn.

A boy of sixteen such summers trundled his wheelbarrow along a stony, rutted path. His tattered woolen tunic and leggings were scarcely enough to keep the morning chill at bay. To his left was a dense, shadowed forest. To his right, a steep, jagged cliff dropped away to a rocky, wave-battered shore.

This land was called Britain by some, Wales by others, but the boy, who was called Corwin, didn't consider himself a vassal of any kingdom. It was the year four hundred and twenty-five, but Corwin wasn't a cleric who kept track of the calendar. On this day, he was a simple beachcomber and hoped that was all anyone who saw him would think of him. For there was a price on his head, and his best hope was to avoid recognition.

Corwin's wheelbarrow sounded too loud to his ears in

the predawn stillness. He wished he had thought to muffle the wheels with straw. The only other sounds were the roar of the waves below and the cries of the seagulls above. Those and a certain cawing raven that circled high over Corwin's head, a black shadow against the blacker sky, making raucous noise as if to mock him.

The raven was called Nag, and in Corwin's opinion it was an appropriate name—nagging seemed to be all that the annoying bird ever did. It had belonged to his old mentor, Fenwyck, and now that Fenwyck was gone, the bird followed Corwin. But it wouldn't take food from Corwin's hand, and it never rested on his shoulder. It was almost as though the raven blamed Corwin for his mentor's death.

At last, through the mist, Corwin saw what he was looking for—a lone, ancient, twisted and weathered cypress tree standing at the edge of the cliff. Its bent branches extended out over the precipice like an aged widow reaching for a love lost at sea. Some called it a "witch tree," and there were many stories of how it had once been a sorceress enchanted by some god or demon. Corwin just thought of it as a lucky break. He had more practical uses for the tree than stories.

He stopped his wheelbarrow by the withered roots, as

he had for many mornings in a row now, and pulled out of the barrow a long length of rope, a leather sack, and a wooden pulley. Corwin easily shimmied up the tree's twisted trunk and crawled out onto the thickest branch to hang the block pulley, avoiding looking down at the drop to the sharp rocks below. He threaded the rope through the wheel of the pulley and slithered back down the tree, holding both ends of the line.

Back on the ground, Corwin tied one end of the rope securely to the wheelbarrow. Then he kicked it off the cliff. As it swung out into the air, Corwin carefully let the rope slip through his callused hands, lowering the barrow down to the shore.

Now came the hard part. Corwin tied the end of the rope he still held around his waist and began the dangerous climb down the cliff face. The rocks were slick with dew and damp and sea spray. There had been a storm the night before, which made his footing treacherous, but his spirits hopeful. Storm waves always brought more shells and other treasures to the shore. In the past, he had found such wonders as a wooden shoe, hollow balls of green and blue glass, a carved flute of whalebone, and a very strange hairy nut that contained white meat and water. And for every ten buckets of shells Corwin gathered, the old blind button-maker Henwyneb would . pay him a penny.

My life has certainly become lowly, Corwin thought, as his hand nearly lost its grip on a slippery rock. He had known better times. How he and Fenwyck, the only guardian Corwin had ever known, used to dazzle the crowds at the county fairs. Fenwyck styled himself a sorcerer and illusionist, and the pennies flowed in amazement at his tricks. Of course, some of the pennies would flow from their unknowing owners' pockets and purses as Fenwyck and Corwin walked among the crowd. There had been more than a bit of thief in Fenwyck's conniving nature, and that had proved his undoing.

If only you hadn't seen that little silver chalice in the castle, Corwin thought. *Fenwyck, why'd you have to get yourself killed over a pretty bauble and turn me into a hunted man?* But because Fenwyck had saved Corwin's life, in the end, Corwin felt more guilt and sorrow than anger.

It isn't like I haven't known worse times, as well, he reminded himself, as he just barely stopped a sliding fall by grabbing a root that stuck out from the cliff. Corwin's earliest memories were of wandering alone in the woods. He'd managed—his senses had kept him out of the worst danger, and he'd grown up strong. He'd manage again, somehow.

At last, Corwin reached the bottom of the cliff. He untied the rope from his waist and untied the other end from the wheelbarrow. There was enough sand between the rocks that he was able to maneuver the barrow along without much trouble. With a now much-practiced eye, Corwin scanned the shore, looking for anything out of the ordinary, anything that wasn't driftwood, sand, or stone.

Unfortunately, the storm didn't seem to have brought him any special treasures this morning. But there were plenty of shells, and Corwin dutifully filled the leather sack. He also picked up mussels and put them in his pockets so that he might have a meal later in the day. Nag, the raven, helped himself to some shellfish on the sand, as well as whatever unlucky fish had washed ashore.

Time passed until the sky was bright and pink with the coming dawn. The large leather sack was now full, and Corwin trundled the barrow back to the rope and pulley. He tied one end of the rope around the top of the leather sack. Next he hauled on the other end of the line, hoisting the sack high in the air, nearly to the overhanging branch of the tree above, then found a rock to securely weight his end of the rope. It was a nuisance, but Corwin had learned with practice that it was best to raise the shells first and climb up after, rather than try to scale the cliff with a heavy sack on his back. He could grab the sack with a long, hooked stick once he was at the top, then lower another empty sack for a second round of gathering.

The rope was secured and, with a sigh, Corwin approached the cliff for his climb. It was hard to live each day by the whims of fate. But he didn't know what else to do. Fenwyck had taught Corwin little except how to fool folk with clever tricks and steal from them, and Corwin was in enough trouble as it was without getting his hand caught in someone's purse strings.

There were other lands and other peoples, he knew, but Corwin preferred living alone in a cave in the woods to living among strangers whose ways he wouldn't know and whose tongue he couldn't speak. Besides, Corwin didn't even know how far the king's men would be seeking for him.

If only I could have a useful *vision, one that tells me what I should do*, he thought. Corwin had been afflicted with occasional, strange storms of hallucination ever since he could remember, but they had never been of any use to him. They were never *about* him, only of people and events far away in time or place. A witch-woman had once told him he had the gift of prophecy, but Corwin thought of it more as a curse than a gift. Fenwyck, of course, had tried to make money off it, proclaiming Corwin as a wise seer. Corwin had quickly learned to lie whenever he was called upon to foresee someone's future—especially when he was given a vision. *If only I'd been able to lie to the king,* Corwin thought. *Maybe Fenwyck would've lived, and I wouldn't have to hide from the world now.*

Suddenly Corwin heard a raucous cawing from behind him. Talons plucked at his back and shoulder, and black wings beat him about the head. "Nag! Nag! What's the matter with you? Are you insane?" Corwin flailed his arms to shoo the raven away, but the creature wouldn't be dissuaded. "What? What? What *is* it?"

Nag rose into the air and flew off at great speed to an outcropping headland to the west, circled around several times, and flew back with screeching cries.

"You've found something," Corwin murmured. Then, with greater hope than he'd felt all morning, he exclaimed, "You've found something!" Leaving the cliff side, Corwin bounded over the rocks, following the excited bird.

He sidled along the edge of the projecting rocks, careful

not to slip into the foaming water that sucked at his feet. Corwin rounded the headland to see a portion of beach he hadn't investigated before. And something else.

Nag circled over a long, brown-and-green . . . thing that lay on the sand. It glistened too much to be a log. It was too compact to be seaweed. And it had huge golden eyes that stared back at him.

"A leviathan," Corwin whispered. "A monster of the sea."

Slowly, cautiously, he crept up on the creature, hoping it was dead. He had seen a small beached whale once. He had even tried to get a beached porpoise back out into the water one time, not that it had done any good—he knew the poor, confused creature would just beach itself again. He'd seen many large fish washed ashore. But this thing was neither whale nor porpoise nor fish.

A pack of seagulls were circling the leviathan, occasionally swooping down to take pecks at it. The creature didn't move. *If I'm lucky, it's dead*, Corwin thought. He walked up to it and shooed the gulls away.

Crouching down, Corwin picked up a stick of driftwood and poked gently at the thing. It had tentacles! Corwin had seen octopuses before—merchants from distant lands sold them, salted and dried, in the port markets. But those were no larger than his hand, and this creature was huge, longer than he was tall. And this thing had ten tentacles, not eight. The large, golden eyes were clouded and didn't follow his movements. *Dead, or so close to it that it barely matters*, Corwin thought.

There was a curious, not-pleasant smell around the creature, and Corwin noticed that the sand was black with its blood. The long, bulbous head had deep gashes in the skin that had clearly not been made by the hungry gulls. *Maybe the storm dashed it against the rocks?* Corwin wondered. But his instinct told him the creature had been in a fight. And had lost.

Corwin shivered, then stood up again, wondering what he could possibly do with this find. He couldn't drag the whole thing back with him and hoist it up the cliff. If he just cut off part of it, no one would believe him when he described the size—and besides, he couldn't show his face in public anyway, so who would he tell? Blind Henwyneb the button-maker would only think Corwin was playing a joke.

Corwin doubted the creature would be any good to eat. As hungry as he was, not having eaten that morning, Corwin's stomach still turned at the thought. He walked back and forth along the leviathan's length, as he considered what to do. The morning tide was coming in, lapping at the creature's tentacles, making them move with a semblance of life.

Corwin saw something glinting amid the tentacles, something silvery. He had heard stories about where pearls came from. What might a creature this size produce? Corwin knelt down, but he couldn't escape the fear that, should he reach toward it, one of the huge tentacles might wrap around his arm or his head and crush him. He took a deep breath and watched the water. The wavelets came in, the wavelets went out. He mentally timed it so that he could grab the shiny thing while the water receded, so that the tentacles wouldn't be moving. He took a deep breath.

The wavelets went out. He reached in among the rubbery, blubbery tentacles, and his hand closed on the silvery object. Corwin pulled it out quickly and tucked it into his lap before the water came in again. He let his breath out in a relieved sigh. But the relief faded as he realized that the water wasn't coming back in.

Every fiber of his being tingled with fear. He could no longer hear the waves or the rush of the seafoam. There were no more cries from seagulls overhead. All the sounds of the world seemed to have vanished. There was only . . . silence.

Corwin turned his head to gaze at the ocean. It, too, had . . . stopped. And it was no longer the familiar dark green-blue tipped with white of a normal sea. The water had turned a deep blood red. Corwin swallowed hard. "What is this?" he whispered. "What did I do?"

With horror, he stared as the water began to return to the shore. But it didn't flow as the sea normally would. It began to crawl, like a living thing, creeping up the beach. Tendrils extended from the edge of the water, like fingers, feeling their way along the strand, searching. One of the tendrils touched the tip of one of the leviathan's tentacles.

Suddenly a ghastly screech tore through the air, exploding on Corwin's ears, as if an uncountable host of tiny mouths wailed in a horrible, triumphant chorus. The sound drowned out Corwin's own scream as the gruesome bloodtide began to bulge upward toward the sky. Up and up it rose, stretching into the hideous form of a giant, writhing serpent. The head of the thing formed a gigantic, gaping mouth. And eyes. Eyes that looked down and *saw* Corwin.

Willing his legs to action, Corwin jumped away from the leviathan and staggered back on the beach. Gasping in fear, Corwin leaped over the rocks and stumbled through the water, running for his life. He rounded the headland cliff once more and tore back to where he had left his wheelbarrow. He allowed himself one swift glance back over his shoulder.

It was enough. To his horror, the creature was *pursuing* him. But not by crawling on the land. Somehow the scarlet serpent was flying—wriggling through the air, its back end coiling endlessly out of the sea. *If it's made of the sea*, Corwin thought in terror, *then there may truly be no end to it and no safe distance I can run.*

With the creature right behind him, Corwin reached the barrow and the anchor rope. Hardly thinking, he unwound the anchor rope from the rock and wrapped it around his palm, holding on with all of his strength. Corwin vaulted into the air as the heavy sack of shells plummeted toward the beach. Its counterweight pulled Corwin up, just in time for his ankles to escape the snapping jaws of the sea serpent.

And then, a stroke of good fortune. The monster moved its head a little to the side, just underneath the falling sack of shells. The sack bashed hard onto the creature's head. The serpent exploded in a spray of red droplets onto the rocks below, no more substantial than a summer rain. The sack struck the ground, bursting and sending shells scattering over the strand.

Corwin leapt for the cypress branch, just barely missing getting his hand rammed through the pulley. Shaking and shivering, he slid down the tree trunk and flattened himself on the ground at the cliff top to catch his breath. Shifting forward, he peered over the edge of the cliff, checking to make sure he was safe. And he nearly screamed again.

The red droplets were crawling over the sand and rock, coming back together, recoalescing into the serpent shape. Again it formed eyes and the huge, gaping mouth. It began to slither up the cliff toward him.

It wasn't killed after all! Isn't there anything I can do? Corwin wondered, paralyzed with fear.

Just then, a bright glow filled the air. The first beams of the rising sun penetrated the mist, raced across the surface of the sea and struck the cliff. And the creature.

The serpent screamed and arched its back as if stabbed by a sword. Where the sun touched it, the creature melted as if made of ice. Its blood red color faded to green-gray. The creature washed down onto the shore, flowing outward, its body mere seawater once more.

The water flowed back through the rocks, into the sea. The entire ocean regained its natural color and began its rhythmic movement in and out once more, as Corwin's breathing returned to its natural flow. The familiar roar of the waves returned to match the pounding of his heart.

He sat up. All seemed as it was when he had first come to the shore that morning. Except that his sackful of carefully gathered shells now lay smashed and broken among the rocks below.

Corwin groaned. What demon had sent him such a nightmare? Now he had nothing to show for his pains, not a single shell.

He became aware that he was gripping something in his right hand. Corwin looked down. He was still holding the silvery, glittery thing he had found within the leviathan. Somehow he had held onto it throughout his ordeal.

Corwin held it up and examined it. It *was* a shell, but not like any he had ever seen before. It was spiraled, like a coiled horn—opalescent, glimmering with many colors beneath a silvery sheen. Corwin's right hand itched and he shifted the shell to his left hand. Corwin stared down at his palm. There was a fresh welt in the skin, a welt distinctly in the shape of a sun.

How on earth did that happen? Corwin wondered.

Suddenly he felt a sharp pain in his gut, and the world spun violently around him.

Chapter Two

That red serpent-creature cursed or poisoned me! Corwin thought in horror as he writhed on the ground. The wave of nausea passed for a moment and the dizziness eased, but Corwin suspected he would feel it again.

I have to get to shelter. I can't be found helpless like this. At any moment some fisherman could come along and find me and make himself rich by turning me in.

It had been old, blind Henwyneb who had told Corwin that soldiers of the king's guard had been circulating through Carmarthen, seeking a young man of slender yet muscular build, with brown hair and gray eyes. Apparently there were even posters put up in the center of town that had been painstakingly drawn by monks. Corwin had been tempted to go look at these drawings to see how closely men who had never seen him had captured his likeness. But fear and common sense had won the argument with curiosity and vanity, and Corwin had stayed away from town.

Why am I so distracted? Corwin wondered. *I need to find shelter, and soon.* Still clutching the opalescent shell, Corwin grabbed onto the withered cypress tree and pulled himself up. He stood, wavering, and then loped into the shadows of the nearby forest.

No sooner had he gotten among the trees than another wave of nausea struck him. Doubled over, Corwin saw a cluster of holly bushes beneath an ancient oak. He staggered to the oak, slipped into a hollow between the bushes, and curled up tightly upon a bed of leaves. The dizziness overwhelmed him so completely that he prayed he wouldn't have to move again.

If this is just a fever, Corwin thought hopefully, *then maybe it'll be gone in a day. I've suffered worse. But if it's poison or a curse, then I could die right here. Well, if I die, maybe I'll meet my master Fenwyck in whatever afterlife has let him in. But this pain is so bad! If I'm going to die, then please make it soon.*

A violent shudder shook him, and then an uneasy peace stole over him. Visions appeared before his mind's eye. *Oh, no, now is not the time. . . .*

But these were not like the visions of prophecy that had visited Corwin before. For these sights were definitely about *him.*

He saw a shoreline that was not the rocky coast he had just left, but felt deeply familiar. And a woman's face. She had honey-brown hair, and gray eyes like his, and it was the most beautiful face he had ever known. Tears flowed from Corwin's eyes. She had been his mother—he knew that in his soul, and yet he had had no waking memory of her. Corwin felt a sudden, painful loneliness and he longed for the woman to be near, to comfort him. The vision faded and he cried out, "No! Don't go, don't go!" A memory smote him of the woman sleeping and himself trying to wake her. But she wouldn't waken.

Corwin began to sob, but he felt the peculiar peacefulness steal over his mind again, as if someone outside himself was trying to calm him. *Could it be my mother's spirit has come down from heaven to ease my suffering?*

Before he could seek to learn the answer, more memories swarmed into his mind. This time he was back in the forest, wandering amid brooks and branches, watching deer and foxes and rabbits, almost as if he had been one of them. Indeed, he'd felt as though he were one with them, for he had dined on berries and wild apples and fish as the bears do, and nibbled on mushrooms and dandelion leaves as the rabbits do. He had swum in the forest streams and pools and could often stay under for minutes at a time, staring at the fishes and frolicking with the otters. Other than the loneliness and occasional periods of hunger, those had been pleasant days for Corwin.

And then came Fenwyck. In his mind's eye, Corwin saw Fenwyck (looking quite a bit younger than the last time Corwin had seen him) bending down and saying, "What *am* I going to do with you? You're a little animal, wild as a fox cub." Fenwyck was wearing the spangled and fringed purple robe "as worn by the high sorcerer-priests of Hamurabia!" as Fenwyck would proclaim.

The old liar. There probably never was a Hamurabia, Corwin thought, but fondly.

More memories came. Fenwyck walking beside him down some dusty road. "I will call you . . . Corwin," he was saying. "For Corwin is near the Roman word for raven, and you are as wild and smart as any raven. You pick up words like one, too." Corwin hadn't minded being named after a bird. That is, until Nag came along.

"D'you like him?" Fenwyck was saying, in a memory from a few years later, pointing at a black bird sitting on his shoulder. "I won him off an old one-eyed man at a game of bones last night. The man must have been daft— when I'd told him he'd lost, he claimed to have no money and gave me the bird instead. And then he laughed as if it had been the biggest jest on me. Well, we'll show him, won't we? We'll make the raven part of our act."

The bird, which was very dubious-looking, had refused to learn any tricks or mimic any words. But for reasons unclear to Corwin, Fenwyck had kept it anyway, naming it Nag. Sometimes Corwin had thought Fenwyck was fonder of the raven than of him.

Corwin shuddered again, and his memories flashed forward another few years. Fenwyck returning to their hovel drunk and reeking of ale, yelling at Corwin for chores not done or lessons not learned. A stick pulled down from a hook on the wall—stinging blows across Corwin's back and face. He curled up more tightly against these memories and they, too, faded.

Why am I remembering all this? Corwin wondered. *I've heard that before they die, men see their whole lives pass before their eyes. Does this mean I'm about to die?*

But he continued to fall into another vision. A pleasant one, this time. His first county fair! What a wonder that had been. Booths with heavenly smells of baked bread and meat pies and sweet cakes that would make his mouth water. Horses and cattle and pigs and ducks, all traded, bought and sold. Weavers had cloth to sell, and farmers brought their fresh harvest. Barrel makers and blacksmiths, carpenters and tinkers all plied their trade. Minstrels played on lute and flute, and country girls danced to the drum and tambor. To Corwin it had seemed all the wonders of the human world could be found at the fair.

"Quit gawking, boy," Fenwyck had said, shaking Corwin's shoulder. "And mind the purses that pass by, at about your eye level. Note the ones whose owners are inattentive and haven't closed them fully. Note the ones that hang too loose from their owners' belts. Remember what I've taught you—bump, dip in, grab what's easiest, and get away. Don't be greedy, for that's the downfall of every pickpocket and pinch-purse there ever was."

Fenwyck, if only you'd followed your own advice, Corwin thought.

Another year later, and they were standing on a stage of uneven wood planks, Fenwyck holding up his arms and proclaiming, "Behold! Upon this very platform, my lords and ladies, I shall demonstrate the mysteries of the ancients, wonders of far distant lands, secrets even the Romans did not know!"

Corwin would be pushed forward then, to stare out at a crowd of goggling peasants.

"Behold, good citizens, the Wild Boy of Caledonia!

Found in the forest, able to speak only the tongues of animals. Said to have been the get of a princess and a demon. Watch as I place this fish into this barrel. The boy will catch it with his teeth, with no need to come up for air!"

Corwin had easily been able to do it, of course. He had always been astonished at the gasps of amazement he heard from the crowd.

"Behold!" Fenwyck would go on, "I will now conjure fire!"

On any bright day, Fenwyck could do this trick. For he had within his sleeve a burning glass—a little round lens. Fenwyck would hold up his arms dramatically and at the right angle and pronounce some impressive-sounding mumbo jumbo. Sure enough, the scrap of paper or cloth on the table in front of him would soon burst into flame. And the crowd would burst into applause.

Then came the fateful day when a woman, besotted with Fenwyck's sorcerous abilities, had rushed forward and said, "Oh, wise seer, can you please foretell my future?"

Fenwyck had been nonplussed and he hesitated. "Well, I—I don't have all of my necessary equipment with me. . . ."

Corwin had stepped up to the edge of the stage then, for he *knew*; he suddenly could see a part of her future, as if a bit of the thread of Fate had become a scroll that he could read. "You're going to have a child," he told her. "A boy child."

The woman smiled radiantly. "Yes? Yes?"

"But he . . . will be missing some fingers and toes," Corwin went on. "And he will be blind. And he will die before he is a year old."

The woman's smiles turned to a sneer of disgust and horror. "What? How dare you tell me such a thing! You disgusting little creature!"

She had rushed at Corwin, and Fenwyck had intervened to stand between them. "He—he means nothing, madam. He was making a joke, a horrible joke, to be sure, but pay him no mind." Fenwyck then dragged Corwin behind the stage for a whacking. "You . . . must . . . only . . . tell . . . people . . . nice . . . things!" Fenwick had declared in rhythm with his blows.

"But it's *true!*" Corwin had protested.

"I don't care if it's true!" Fenwyck declared. "The truth is not going to make us rich!"

Corwin had been very careful from then on to tell only the good things that he saw. Although when a powerful vision would strike him, Corwin would not be able to lie and therefore would say nothing at all.

A quiet memory next—sitting next to Fenwyck before a campfire, eating some smoked venison and drinking watered wine. "Fenwyck, who were my parents? Was my mother really a princess and my father a demon?"

Fenwyck had only looked at him and said, "Your mother would want you to think of her as a good woman. And that's all I will say on the matter."

More memories, more county fairs. Corwin grew and could do sleight of hand as well as, if not better than, Fenwyck. He learned to be glib-tongued and strong as Fenwyck became old and tired. But with all of their skill and tricks and occasional thieving, they still had not become rich. Fenwyck's beard had become gray, his "Hammurabian" robe became tattered, and their perform- ances had become stale. Corwin had thought, guiltily, of setting out on his own and would have done so, except that he knew no other life.

In a moment of clarity, Corwin's mind returned to his surroundings. He was still lying on the bed of leaves beneath the holly bushes and the oak tree. From the angle of the sunlight filtering down through the forest canopy, he could see it was now midday. *I have journeyed through the years of my past and the sun has journeyed high in the sky. Is this still the same day as when I fell here, I wonder?*

Why doesn't my mind feel like my own? Has the red sea creature somehow captured my thoughts to play with?

At a familiar raucous cry, Corwin peered up at the branches overhead. Nag was stalking back and forth along the lowermost oak bough, tilting his head this way and that as he regarded Corwin on the ground.

"I'm ill, you stupid bird," Corwin grumbled. "If you want to be useful, go get me some food, or a wine flask, or at least a water bag."

Nag extended his neck and opened his beak wide with an accusatory "Raaawk!" as if to say, "Who are you calling stupid?" Then the bird hopped down onto the leaves beside Corwin and began gently pecking at the silver shell in his hands.

"You leave that alone," Corwin said, pulling the shell tighter to his chest. "It's the only fortune I have left. Just go away, if you won't help."

Nag ruffled his feathers and shook his head and stalked away, muttering in incomprehensible raven-talk.

"And don't—oh, Gods!" Corwin cried as again his mind sank into memories. This time it was the memory he had been dreading.

He slipped back to a time only a few weeks before. Fenwyck and Corwin were strolling through the central square of Carmarthen, debating how to spend their last penny, when they saw townsfolk gathering around a crier. Joining the crowd, Corwin and Fenwyck heard the crier announce:

"Let it be known to all assembled, His Majesty, the mighty and valorous King Vortigern——"

This elicited some snickers from the audience, which the crier ignored.

"——will be holding court in his castle here in Carmarthen for the summer. He will be arriving tonight, so the roads into the city must be cleared for his processional retinue. Any caught blocking the king's passage shall be harshly punished. However, His Royal Majesty wishes to be a bringer of good fortune to the city of Carmarthen. Therefore, those wishing to be in the king's service may find their labor rewarded if they report to the Office of the Royal Steward within the next fortnight."

"Well, what do you think, Fenwyck?" Corwin had asked. "Should we try some honest labor for once?"

"What?" Fenwyck protested. "Scrubbing floors and emptying chamber pots? We haven't sunk that low, lad. Once you begin accepting lesser duties, the greater chances slip away like oil from a leaky barrel."

Corwin rubbed his stomach to quell its rumblings. "If

we don't eat soon, my strength is what's going to be slipping away."

"Be patient," Fenwyck snapped.

"In addition," the crier went on, "His Most High Royal Majesty seeks a particular personage. On the advice of his soothsayers, His Majesty is in search of . . . a visionary boy. Yet this can be no ordinary youth. This must be a boy who has *no* man for a father, and who can see the future with the same clarity as the past. Should such a youth be found and proved worthy, the reward for him and his mother or guardian would include a permanent position in the king's new mountain fortress."

"Well, there you are," Fenwyck said, with a rapturous smile. "It's as though the gods themselves heard and answered our wish. *That* is for us."

"But I *had* a father," Corwin argued. "I just don't know who he was. And you know I don't see the future clearly—"

"Hush!" Fenwyck cut in. "How would the king know that? All we have to do is convince him."

"But—"

"But me no buts, my lad. One does not stand and dither at the gate of Heaven! This is the gateway to greater wealth and comfort than we have ever known. To be permanently installed in court as a Royal Druid? What better location for two connivers like us? There's no greater den of liars than a royal court, I can tell you."

And so the very next morning Fenwyck, with Nag riding on his shoulder, and Corwin had reported to the Office of the Royal Steward. A very dubious lower chamberlain had ushered them into a tapestry-lined waiting room. There, dozens of other townsfolk, men and women, stood anxiously, all with little boys by their sides. The boys had been scrubbed pink and were wearing whatever finery their families could afford. Everyone stared with open distrust and hostility at Fenwyck and Corwin and Nag.

Fenwyck was not going to let any of it bother him, however. He had smiled at all of them grandly and said, "Good morning to you all, gentlemen and ladies."

"You're going to die!" a little redheaded boy burst out, pointing at Fenwyck. His mother hushed him fiercely.

But Fenwyck had patiently retained his smile and crouched down to the boy's eye level. "Of course I am, good young master, as are we all someday. But I fear you'll have to do better than that to impress the king." Nag squawked as if to agree.

Corwin, however, had been more disturbed by the

outburst than his mentor. For Corwin had had disturbing dreams the night before, and he wondered if the little boy might be as prescient as himself.

At last, the door at the end of the waiting chamber had opened, and a dark-bearded man in a beautiful robe of blue silk walked in, bearing a staff topped by a chunk of crystal.

"One of the king's own sorcerers," Fenwyck had whispered in Corwin's ear. "Anguis, I think he calls himself. He attended one of my shows once, before you came along. I tricked him out of ninepence at pick-the-card. Poor fellow was terribly humiliated."

The sorcerer walked slowly among the townsfolk, gazing into the face of each little boy. When one of the adults tried to speak to the sorcerer, Anguis would quell their queries with a solemn glare. The sorcerer himself said nothing, though he paused for long moments when he came to the boy who had told Fenwyck he would die. Then the sorcerer came to Fenwyck himself. "You!" Anguis declared, with a disgusted frown.

"What of it?" Fenwyck had replied. "I have as much right to put forth my claim as any other."

"Him?" the sorcerer asked, pointing at Corwin.

"He fits the requirements. Corwin has no father. You

can ask anyone, near or far throughout the kingdom, and they will tell you no one knows his sire. They will also tell you of Corwin's demonstrated ability with the Sight."

"Spouting pleasantries to the peasants?" the sorcerer spat.

"He speaks those truths that people will accept," Fenwyck had replied mildly.

"You're frauds, the both of you!"

"Test him for yourself," Fenwyck said softly, "and see."

"Very well," Anguis growled. "Let's get you out of the way first. You might provide His Majesty with some amusement. At least, you had better *hope* he's amused."

The sorcerer had turned, and Fenwyck and Corwin followed him through the ornate carved door at the end of the antechamber.

The throne room was not what Corwin would have expected. Because King Vortigern had only just arrived, the hall was in disarray. Servants were everywhere, hanging up tapestries, arranging chairs, assembling the dais, rolling out carpets. The king himself stood in the center of it all, giving directions, lending a nod of approval or a dismissive wave of his hand to whatever he was shown.

King Vortigern wasn't what Corwin had expected, either. For one thing, he was shorter than Corwin and younger than Fenwyck, with a fat face. If it hadn't been for the gold circlet bearing a single sapphire resting on his head and the people bowing whenever they went past him, Corwin wouldn't have thought that Vortigern looked kingly at all.

"Majesty," said the sorcerer escorting them, "here are the first petitioners for your boy seer." He bowed and then whispered something in Vortigern's ear. Corwin had the impression he wasn't saying anything good.

Fenwyck, meanwhile, dropped to his knees and pulled hard on Corwin's sleeve until Corwin did the same. "O, great King," Fenwyck intoned. "O, mighty conqueror of Britain from whom all mercies and justice flow, O——"

"Yes, yes, yes," Vortigern said impatiently. "Get up, get up, the both of you. Let's get this done with quickly, shall we?" Vortigern waved for them to follow him and strode over to a chair in a corner of the huge chamber. There he sat and crossed one leg over the other. "So. Fenwyck, Magus of Hammurabia, is it?" He cocked his brow in disbelief. "And Master Corwin. My adviser tells me you are frauds. What do you have to say for yourselves?"

Corwin had almost been prepared to like Vortigern, given his informality. But Vortigern looked on them with the cold, calculating gaze of someone who sees other people as mere nuisances to be dealt with. *There won't be any mercy or justice from this man.*

"I say," Fenwyck stated, "that you should hear us out before you judge us, Majesty."

Nag squawked again, and Corwin had the distinct impression that the raven didn't like Vortigern, either.

"Who said you could bring a bird into my throne room?" Vortigern demanded, his ruddy face reddening further.

"Nag is my familiar, Majesty," Fenwyck said with mock hurt pride. "I couldn't possibly appear on so important an occasion without him."

Vortigern wrinkled his nose in disgust. "Well, see that it doesn't . . . drop anything on the carpets. I've had them imported at great expense from Persia."

"Of course not, Majesty."

Two young men walked up to Vortigern. "Father," said one of them, "Faustus here says there isn't going to be a boar hunt today!"

Vortigern shut his eyes firmly. "That's right, my son. I have a somewhat more urgent matter to attend to at this moment."

"What? You can't be serious, Father. Have your sorcerers truly convinced you that your tower will only be saved with a sacrificial lamb?"

Corwin stiffened. Who, exactly, was the lamb to be sacrificed? He looked closer at the prince, who seemed just a couple of years older than him. The prince glanced back, his stare making Corwin feel uncomfortably like a duck hanging in the marketplace to be bought for someone's dinner.

"Wait," the other man, Faustus, said. Corwin switched his gaze to him, taking in his fox face and brushy mustache. "Didn't I see you two at the county fair in Cardiff last year?" Faustus continued, stepping toward Corwin. "You told some poor wench that she would have the love of her dreams. The annoying creature pursued me for weeks after."

"It's . . . possible, my lord," Corwin murmured, bowing.

The prince walked up to Corwin and inspected him closely. "Aren't you a little old for this role?"

"He is big for his age, Highness," Fenwyck said.

"Vortimer," King Vortigern sighed, "if you don't intend to be useful, will you and Faustus kindly go amuse yourselves elsewhere?"

"Nay, Father. We want to see the look on his face when you order him cast into the dungeons." Prince Vortimer and Lord Faustus moved to a nearby pillar and casually leaned against it.

"As you will," King Vortigern said, "but I may let them go free just to spite you. Now," he said, turning back to Fenwyck and Corwin, "here is the matter. I have been trying to have a new tower built in this castle— something tall, so that I might have a good view of the sea, and strong, so that Castle Carmarthen might have a stronger defense. But every time work begins on the tower, it collapses."

Maybe you should pick a new architect and head mason, Corwin thought.

"And before you tell me I should choose a new architect," King Vortigern went on, "let me say that I have done this already, with the same result. Now. My advisers tell me there is a supernatural basis for the collapse, but it is beyond their skill to see the cause."

"These are the same advisers," Prince Vortimer interrupted, "who instructed him to hold a peace conference with the Saxons and Norsemen in the middle of Stonehenge, and you know how well *that* turned out."

Corwin had, in fact, heard the bards sing of how King Vortigern had been driven from the standing stones by barbarians wielding axes, but he thought it would be better not to say anything.

"Vortimer, I repeat, if you aren't going to be useful . . . "

"I apologize, Father. I shall hold my peace. For now."

What a strange royal family, Corwin thought, *where the son is rude to his father and the father doesn't even act like a king*. Corwin had heard some bards, speaking in whispers lest they be heard, who said that King Vortigern had not come by his crown honestly. Vortigern was to have been merely a guardian for King Constans, who, strangely but conveniently, had fallen ill and died at a young age. Vortigern had declared himself the only reasonable person to take the crown, as Constans's brothers, Uther Pendragon and Ambrosius Aurielanus, were away in France.

Neither Corwin nor Fenwyck had paid much attention to politics. "One king is much like another," Fenwyck had often said. But that day, facing the king, Corwin suddenly wished he knew more.

"My advisers," King Vortigern went on, "say that only a boy who has no father will have the Sight to know why my tower keeps collapsing. Do you fit that description, Master Corwin?"

"I have known no father, Majesty," Corwin replied honestly. "Only my guardian, Fenwyck, has raised me."

"And when he was given to me," Fenwyck added, "his mother didn't say anything about a father."

"Hmmm. Sounds like mincing words to me," King Vortigern said. "Nonetheless—"

But he was drowned out by loud shouting. Anguis was arguing with two other long-beards, one in a deep red robe with a matching floppy hat, and the other in forest green with a leather skullcap. "You should have informed us at once!" Red Floppy Hat was saying.

"But I tell you, they're mere thieves and cheats!" Anguis said. "I can't believe you take this at all seriously!"

"Shut up, all of you!" King Vortigern roared, and the three advisers all turned and bowed to him sheepishly. He motioned for them to come over, and all three sorcerers shuffled up to his chair. "What's the matter here?"

"Majesty," said Leather Skullcap, "we cast the bones at dawn and the auguries have indicated that this one may be more than he appears."

Corwin liked the way these men looked at him least of all. They seemed to regard him with a mixture of hope, awe, and fear that made Corwin want to flee the room.

"Well, that's what I'm trying to find out, isn't it?" Vortigern snapped. "Now," he turned back to face Fenwyck and Corwin, "I'm running out of patience. Can you tell me what's knocking down my tower?"

Corwin swallowed hard and dearly wished to be

elsewhere. He tried to think of some impressive mumbo jumbo that the king would want to hear, maybe something about using the stones of Stonehenge itself to build the tower, or—

A blinding headache struck him between the eyes and Corwin fell to his knees. *Oh no, not a real one!* But the vision came upon him and he couldn't stop it. Corwin grabbed the hair on either side of his head and groaned.

And now, lying beneath the holly bushes and the oak tree, Corwin groaned aloud as well. *Why am I seeing this? Why do I have to relive it? Is this my punishment for being a coward? Why won't it stop?*

But the memory continued on without mercy, and with total clarity.

"What is it?" Vortigern demanded. "What are you seeing?"

In the throes of his vision, Corwin couldn't lie. "Two . . . two dragons. One is white and one is red. Their great wings are furled; they look like . . . like roses or cabbages. The dragons are fighting . . . a great battle. Their roars shake the ground. The lashing of their tails makes the earth tremble! No tower can withstand it. There is . . . there is a bear, running toward us, across the ocean. The sun rides on his shoulder but he brings the storm! A crown falls. . . . The bear cub will bring peace, but it must be brought through treachery and deceit. . . ."

"Enough!" King Vortigern bellowed, rising to stand over Corwin. "A crown falls. . . . Know you that it is treason to speak of the death of the king? And how *dare* you speak of peace brought through treachery and deceit!"

"No," Corwin protested, still curled up on the floor. "It may not mean you, Your Majesty! My visions are often of lands far away, or times far off in the future. You can't assume that—"

"How *dare* you tell me what to assume!"

"Well, well, look what *I've* found," Prince Vortimer said, holding tightly onto Fenwyck's wrist. They were both standing by a stack of opened crates. "While all of you were watching the whelp, I found his guardian filching the silverware." Clutched in Fenwyck's fist was a small silver chalice.

"I was merely admiring it!" Fenwyck protested.

Oh no, Fenwyck, no. Not now, Corwin had thought with a sinking heart.

"Aye, and you so flattered it with your favor," said the prince, "that the cup slipped into your sleeve to go home with you."

"It slipped from my fingers—" Fenwyck began.

"Enough!" roared Vortigern again. "You have dishon-ored my court. You have spoken treason. You shall both be put to death for your insolence. Guards!"

To Corwin's astonishment, Fenwyck did the long-practiced twist-pulling of his arm to release himself from the prince's grasp. Then, just as though it were another county fair and he'd been caught pinching pennies, Fenwyck threw down the stack of crates to trip the prince and dashed past Corwin yelling, "Run, lad!"

Then Corwin was on his feet and running for the door. But the throne room was huge and there was much ground to cover, and he was still weak and dizzy from his vision. Swords sprouted from the hands of every noble-man present, and armed men came in through every side door. Corwin slid on a carpet that had just been placed down, sliding under blades aimed at his middle. He leaped onto a table that was dropped by its carriers and kicked it over into the path of his pursuers. Grabbing a rope that dangled from a banner hanging in the middle of the hall, he swung over the heads of three men trying to capture him. Corwin dropped beside the carved door just ahead of Fenwyck. The latch stuck for one second—one second too long. Corwin opened the door just as two guardsmen reached Fenwyck.

Fenwyck grabbed the door frame and hung on as if he were Samson, standing between the guards and Corwin. "Run, boy! Run! Ahhhgh!"

Corwin tore through the antechamber, past the wide-eyed boys and their mothers, out into the courtyard and through the castle gate itself. He had run into the forest as fast as he could go and hid there, sick with shame and fear. It had been two days before Corwin had ventured close enough to Carmarthen to hear and see what had happened to Fenwyck. The old conniver had been put in an iron cage and exposed on the castle walls for all to see, after being flogged and stabbed with swords. Even so, it had taken Fenwyck five days to die. At his death, Nag had returned to find Corwin in the woods and shadowed him thereafter, like his conscience.

Tears flowed down Corwin's cheeks as he lay on the bed of leaves beneath the oak tree. "Why are you making me see all these things?" Corwin asked whatever deity or devil was forcing the memories to run through his mind. "What was I supposed to do? Fight off a whole castle? Die alongside him?" Corwin rubbed his nose on his sleeve and sat up.

The illness had subsided and the strange peace again

returned. The sun was now low in the sky. It was late afternoon.

His stomach rumbled and Corwin realized that he hadn't eaten anything yet that day. Sensations pressed upon his mind once more, but these weren't like his memories. He felt—sand. He heard the sea. He saw the beach where the tentacled leviathan lay . . . only he wasn't seeing these things through his memories of the morning, but as they might look now, in late afternoon. He saw hands that weren't his own—they were slim and tapered feminine hands. He saw an old man with a fishtail instead of legs and felt deep sorrow.

Corwin shook his head violently to clear these strange new visions. It worked, but some of his nausea returned. *Enough! I'm losing my mind. But I will definitely go crazy with hunger if I don't get something to eat.* Corwin pulled himself up and found he could stand.

Henwyneb has skills with herbal tinctures, Corwin thought. *Maybe he has a cure for this strange ailment. Or at least this pretty shell could buy me some soup from his kettle.* The thought of food spurring him on, Corwin staggered out of the forest and headed for the old blind button-maker's cottage as fast as he could go.

Chapter Three

It seemed to take forever to walk down the rutted, muddy road to Henwyneb's hovel. It wasn't that the road was unknown to him—Corwin had walked down it many times in the past month, usually carrying heavy bags of shells for Henwyneb to buy. Now he carried only one shell, yet his pace was slow, so slow. His strange ailment had subsided, but it had left him weak and weary.

But there was another cause as well—his thoughts were now constantly distracted. He was regarding the most ordinary things, such as an oak tree, a flower, a butterfly, or a colorful rock, as if he were a newborn baby seeing these things for the first time. He would see a bluebird fluttering in the treetops, or hear the song of a meadowlark, or the humming of a bumblebee and part of his mind would ask, "What is that? What is that?" as a child who has newly learned speech will pester its mother.

It wasn't that he couldn't remember anything. He could answer himself easily, and he knew as much as he ever did of the names of trees and flowers and birds. In a way, it was a gift to see all these things anew and wonder at them. But it was frightening as well.

Am I so changed by this illness that I will never see the world the same way again? Corwin wondered. *Is this another sign of madness?* Worse yet, he worried that he would be so distracted that danger could overtake him. A contingent of royal guards might easily capture him while he was busy admiring the patterns on a pretty stone.

At last Corwin came to a familiar bend in the road and a short path that led to a small, thatched hovel in a clearing. To one side of the path was an herb garden, which was lush with aromatic plants. Once Corwin had asked old Henwyneb how he could garden when blind. The button-maker had described in loving detail the feel of the earth, the different patterns of each herb's leaves, and their scent when a stem or leaf is crushed. Corwin had thought such sensations the fancies of an old man, but now he could *see* each subtle difference in the patterns of the leaves, and the rich complexity of the aroma of the garden made him want to fall to his knees in awe.

Before he could be caught in thrall with the wonders of the herb garden, Corwin hastened to the cottage door and knocked.

"Enter," Henwyneb called from inside.

Corwin pushed the door open and went in. The dark interior was lit only by a tiny window covered with oiled paper and the fire in the hearth. The aroma of stew from the kettle on the grate was enticing enough to make Corwin's mouth water and his stomach rumble.

"Ah," Henwyneb went on, "I smell the sea upon you. Either you are Stephen the fisherman or you are my mysterious young shell-gatherer come to sell me your latest treasures from the shore."

As the old man came shuffling out of the shadows, Corwin was again entranced, now by the pattern of lines and wrinkles around Henwyneb's pale, milky eyes and nearly toothless mouth. *What is that, what is that?* the insistent questioner in his mind asked, and Corwin had to answer, *It is the face of a man who has lived many years, laughed much laughter, and smiled many smiles, though his eyes are no longer of use.*

"Why don't you speak, visitor? Is . . . something the matter?" Henwyneb asked.

"No, Henwyneb," Corwin answered. "Your second guess was right. But I only have one treasure to offer, and I'll give it freely in exchange for some of your stew and a little medicine."

"Ah. Been a while since your last meal, has it? Well, a meal I will gladly give you. As for the medicine, it will depend upon what you need. Let me see this treasure you have and I will consider the matter."

Corwin no longer even thought it was strange that the blind man spoke of "seeing." He had watched Henwyneb discern more with the touch of his hands than most men could do with their sight. "Here it is." Corwin handed the opalescent shell to Henwyneb, feeling a strange reluctance to let go of it.

"Hmmm." Henwyneb's hands caressed the shell as if it were a precious object. "Unusual, indeed. Most rare. Are you certain you wish to part with it?"

"Um, well . . . "

"As I thought. We will discuss any such trades later. First, let's get some dinner into you. Your belly's complaints are deafening me." Henwyneb put the shell up on an already cluttered shelf and went to the hearth. With hands long accustomed to where everything was placed, Henwyneb took a ladle from a rack beside the hearth and a wooden bowl from the shelf above it. As he ladled the stew from the kettle into the bowl, Corwin sat down on one of the two stools in the room, nearly drooling with his desire to taste the stew. His mind was torn between the part asking, "What is that, what is that?" and his stomach saying, "Whatever it is, give it to me! Now!"

Henwyneb held out the bowl and Corwin greedily took it, not caring that he spilled a few scalding drops on his breeches. He drank the stew down, tasting mussels and scraps of venison and rabbit, carrots and cabbage seasoned with thyme, parsley, and juniper berries. Corwin sighed and leaned back against the wall, closing his eyes. It was the most exquisite meal he had ever tasted. "Ah, this is wonderful," he moaned.

"Hunger does make the best sauce, doesn't it?" Henwyneb said, sitting on the other stool. "Now, tell me about this medicine you need, and whether it's for yourself or someone else."

Corwin took some moments to gobble the rest of the stew down. "Could I have some more stew, first?" he asked.

"By all means," said Henwyneb with an amused smile. "Hearing such praise for my humble cooking, how could I say no?"

Corwin ladled himself a brimming bowlful from the kettle and drank it down again, finding it as delicious as the first. *As madnesses go*, he thought, *this might not be so bad after all*.

At last, with a big sigh, wiping his mouth on his

sleeve, Corwin was ready to set down the bowl and tell Henwyneb everything that had happened to him that morning—of the leviathan on the shore, and the horrible red sea serpent, the strange mark on his hand, and the illness that had struck him afterward.

As Corwin talked, Henwyneb set about heating some water on the hearth. He took down a jar from a nearby shelf and sprinkled some dry herbs into a tiny muslin drawstring bag. Placing this in a mug, he poured hot water into it.

Corwin was finishing with, ". . . and so I finally got up to come here, but I kept noticing everything around me as if I were a child again and . . . what *is* that?" The herbal smell was fascinating to his newly sensitive nose.

"A tisane of marigold leaves and chamomile and mint and . . . oh, a few other things. I find it a soothing tonic for aches and offenses to the stomach, and at least it won't bring you any harm. Until I have a more specific notion of what's wrong with you, this medicine will have to do."

Corwin took the mug in his hands and inhaled the steam. He sipped at the tea, and it tasted mostly like water with leaves steeped in it, but the scent was soothing all by itself. "Thank you, Henwyneb. You're very nice to a stranger."

"Pshaw, you're no stranger, despite the fact that you choose not to tell me your name. You've been in my home before. And I sense that you're as much in need of friends as I am. Now, as to your tale," Henwyneb said, rubbing his cheek thoughtfully, "it's as strange as any I've heard in a long while. And I've heard many, I can assure you, from the sailors and fishermen whom I've met. The sea is a vast, uncharted world, which men can only skim the surface of. What lies beneath, no man can truly know."

He's beginning to sound like Fenwyck, Corwin thought. Although Fenwyck had been the sort of man who believed truth was an annoying obstacle to getting what you wanted; Henwyneb was the sort of man who seemed incapable of speaking anything *but* truth.

The old blind button-maker stood and began to pace the small room. "As to the leviathan, well . . . many a bizarre creature has washed up onto that strand. I have heard tales that would make you shake your head in wonder. Stories of whales larger than this house. Or of the unicorn of the sea, the narwhal, which is very like a whale but has a horn that juts from its forehead."

"As I said," Corwin interrupted, "I've seen whales, and this wasn't like those. It was more like an octopus, but huge. I found that shell I gave you tangled up in its tentacles."

Henwyneb frowned. "The shell may have been within it only coincidentally. Or perhaps the leviathan, too, treasured the object. One sailor I knew told me of an amazing sight he once witnessed. While fishing far from land, he saw a great whale breach from the water. And riding the whale, wrapped around it in a life-strangling grip, was an enormous squid, as large as the whale itself. It was clear to this man that these creatures were fighting to the death, and that the squid would most likely be the victor. But the creatures soon sank beneath the waves, and he never saw them again."

Corwin sat up with interest. "This creature wasn't as big as a whale. It's only a bit longer than I am tall. But there were marks upon it like wounds from a battle!"

"There you are, then," Henwyneb said, smiling. "Perhaps it was a young giant squid. One mystery solved." He sat down again with a heavy sigh. "Now, on to the next. The scarlet serpent you saw coiling out of the sea . . . Sailors whose eyes have been dazed by the ripples of water and the dance of sunlight on the sea have oft thought that floating logs or shadows upon the swells were mighty sea serpents."

"It chased me down and would have killed me, if the sun hadn't struck it!" Corwin said. "Believe me, it was no illusion."

"Well, then." Henwyneb scratched his head in thought. "I once met a fellow from the Far North, a Saxon, who told me of the kraken. This is a monster that lives in the sea and is the cause of maelstroms that drag ships down to their doom. The creature is said to float upon the sea like a woven mat, enticing men to land upon it as though it were an island. It is said to have arms like serpents—perhaps this is what you saw."

"This creature grew eyes and a mouth," said Corwin. "It wasn't just an arm that almost ate me."

"Hmmm. The Northmen also speak of the World Serpent, which dwells at the bottom of the ocean. It was the deadly foe of their thunder god, Thor, but it was said only to rise when the destruction of the world was imminent. I truly hope it was not this that you saw."

Corwin sighed. "All these stories don't help me much. I need to know how to kill it or avoid it if it attacks me again."

"But you already know this," said Henwyneb. "The thing was destroyed by sunlight, you say."

Corwin shook his head. "Somehow, I don't think it was really destroyed." The new mind that spoke within his thoughts only confirmed his feeling that the kraken, or whatever it was, would rise again when the sun set.

"Then you must avoid the sea and the dark, 'tis clear," said Henwyneb.

"I wish it were that simple," Corwin said. *What possible life could I live, avoiding men during the day and a monster at night?*

"Surely there is some other occupation you could try than gathering seashells by the seashore?"

"What about the mark on my hand?" Corwin said, changing the subject before Henwyneb could pry further into his circumstances.

"Let me see it." The old man stood and shuffled over. He took Corwin's right hand in both of his and traced the raised mark on Corwin's palm with his fingers. "You're right. . . . it's very like the shape of the sun."

"Do you know what would make a mark like that?"

Henwyneb paused. "No. But do you know much about the Druids?"

"Druids!" Corwin nearly laughed. "They don't tell anyone their secrets. What would those scholars and wizards have to do with me?"

"I only ask because they are said to worship the sun and base their sciences on teachings older than those of the Romans." Henwyneb stood very still for a moment, then walked to the papered window. "You say you see things with new wisdom?"

"Not with new wisdom," Corwin answered, "but with new eyes and senses. It's as if—as if there is another *me* inside, but different somehow." He shook his head. He really *did* sound crazy.

"Hmm. That may prove to be the same thing, in time."

"So you believe this ailment is a blessing, not a curse?"

"As to that, I couldn't say, for wisdom can often prove to be both. The denizens of the sea are often said to be the bringers of gifts—fish that grant wishes. And the merrows."

"What are merrows?" Corwin asked with a frown. So much new information was coming at him, and he had been newly infused with so much curiosity that it was all quite overwhelming.

"The mermen and mermaids who are said to visit our shores. There is a tale of a man named Lutey, who rescued a mermaid from a tide-pool. In gratitude, she gave him the skill and knowledge of healing, which he passed down through his family. Though, as I recall, at the end Lutey had to leave his land-wife and sons and join the mermaid in the sea. And though there are many stories of land people falling in love with merrows, or vice versa, these tales often don't end well for one or the other. And if there are children from these unions, they might be born with a curse upon them, or webbed feet, or scaly skin."

"Your thoughts wander more than mine, old man," Corwin said. "I haven't seen any mermaids." But he did remember the vision from the mind-that-was-not-his of the gray-bearded man with a fin instead of legs. And that *other* sense inside of him—it seemed to itch at the description the button-maker had just given him, as if there were something familiar there. Because of that vision, maybe?

"No one I know has seen any mermaids, either, my boy, but that doesn't prevent their legends from persisting. The sea is so vast that it can contain whole kingdoms of human fancy. And who is to say what does or doesn't exist? Selkies and sea serpents, ghost ships and giants, mysterious islands that appear and disappear. Do you know the tale of Atlantis?"

"No," Corwin said. He noticed that his new inner mind suddenly became very attentive.

"It's a story from the ancient days. Of an island whose people offended the gods and sank into the sea. But it was said the Atlanteans were a great civilization, a people older and wiser than mankind. A Roman centurion I met long ago, who stayed in Wales after his regiment was ordered home, told me of it. He mentioned that there are roads in this land, straight as plumbed lines, connecting landmarks of importance, that were not built by his people. They existed before the Romans arrived. His commander used to joke that the people of Atlantis built them."

Too bad Fenwyck never heard that story, Corwin thought. *He could have made more use of it than of Hammurabia. The wonders of the ancients right under our own noses!* For a moment, Corwin acutely missed the old conniver.

"Ah, but forgive me," Henwyneb said. "These are just prattlings. My mind wanders too freely these days, as you said. These summer evenings are a delight, when the sun lingers late."

Corwin wondered why that should matter to a blind man, but then understood that Henwyneb could feel the warmth upon his face.

Suddenly Henwyneb cocked his head and appeared to be listening to something. "Two horses approaching. Male riders—noblemen, from their speech. Are you expecting others to join you?"

Corwin sat up. "What—?" Then he heard the soft

hoofbeats and men's voices. "No! In fact, I would rather not meet anyone else right now."

"Ah. Then you had better find a place to hide, since they are clearly coming here, and I have no other door but the one they will surely come through."

Corwin spotted a stack of short, stout barrels in one corner. Onto these had been heaped sticks and deer antlers and shells and other materials from which Henwyneb could make buttons. Corwin slipped behind the barrels just as he heard voices coming near the door.

"I must say, this isn't promising," one man was saying. "This looks more like a giant ox-dropping than a house."

"Just what Father's sorcerers suggested we look for. I swear to you, Faustus, his superstitious nature will be the death of him someday. When I'm king, I will see all those sorcerers strangled and hanged by the threads of their pointy caps."

Corwin crouched down lower as he recognized the voices. It was none other than Prince Vortimer and his friend Lord Faustus, both of whom, of course, would recognize Corwin right away.

The door opened and the two young nobles stepped in, without even knocking. "Now you must admit," said Faustus, "that something strange *is* going on with the tower. Just yesterday the third tier of stones fell again, nearly killing one of the workmen."

"Sabotage, probably," said Vortimer. "Father isn't exactly popular with the local people. Or it could be the cisterns and viaducts below the castle that bring water in from the river. You should come explore them with me someday, Faustus, they're huge. But I don't care what they say about Roman architecture—it's not miraculous. You can't build a castle over man-made caverns and lakes that size and not expect some shifting and collapse. I've tried to tell Father this, but does he listen? What *is* that foul smell?"

"I believe it's whatever's in the kettle on the hearth," said Faustus. "Helloooo, is there anyone here?"

Henwyneb shuffled out of the darkness. "Gentlemen, welcome to my humble home," he said, bowing from the waist.

"Gentlemen?" said Prince Vortimer with a sneer. "I will have you know, peasant, that I am a prince of the realm, none other than the firstborn son of King Vortigern himself. On your knees, sirrah, and give me the honors due a prince."

Nasty brute, Corwin thought, his hands clenching into fists at his sides. *He's worse than his father, the king.*

"F-forgive me, Highness," Henwyneb stammered as he slowly lowered himself. "I am blind and could not see who you were."

"Faster, man," Faustus snapped, and he pushed on Henwyneb's shoulders until the button-maker fell to his knees.

Henwyneb cried out in pain. "Have mercy, Highness," he begged. "It is my old joints that prevented me from making haste to do you honors. Forgive me."

Corwin's temple throbbed and he nearly jumped out from his hiding place. *How dare they do this? Just because they're noblemen. They're just big bullies. I wish I could show them.* But Corwin stayed hidden, afraid of being captured. He hated himself for his cowardice.

"Mercy, eh?" Vortimer mocked. "Very well, I shall not have you beheaded. But I will require a tax, a tithe, a fine for your failures. Let me see . . ." The prince glanced around the room. To Corwin's dismay, the prince's gaze fixed upon the shiny shell Corwin had brought. "Ah. This looks interesting. Might have fetched you a penny or three. I'll take this."

There was a tiny wail of fear from the mind within Corwin's mind as Prince Vortimer snatched the shell from the shelf.

"If that is the large, round, spiral shell with a sheen of silver," said Henwyneb, "then it is not mine to give, Highness. It belongs to another."

"You dare to tell me what I can and cannot take?" Vortimer asked, his voice cold.

"It seems this rude lackey would like a beating," suggested Faustus, who, from the cocky grin on his face, was enjoying the prospect.

"No!" Corwin cried, unable to hide any longer. He jumped out of the pile of sticks and antlers, shouting, "Leave him alone!"

The two noblemen stared at him as though he were a jester who had popped out of the earth. Vortimer handed the shell to Faustus and approached Corwin's corner. "Well, well, well," said the prince. "It would appear the soothsayers spoke sooth after all. This is the very scoundrel we've been looking for."

Corwin knew he was too weak to fight, but he didn't have to reveal that to the prince. "Get out! Leave us alone!" he snarled.

"Or you'll . . . what?" asked the prince, coming closer until his face was inches from Corwin's. "If you lay a hand on me, that is treason and punishable by death."

Unfortunately, the prince was right. Corwin knew he

had just ruined whatever hopes he could have for freedom. He tried to put a brave face on it. "I'm already dead if you capture me, aren't I?" he asked. "What do I care if I take you with me?"

"Oooh, this puppy growls fiercely," purred the prince. "I wonder if his bite is as fierce as his bark."

Both Vortimer and Faustus were older, perhaps in their twenties, bigger and stronger than Corwin, and noblemen trained to the sword since they were children. Corwin didn't have a chance. But as Fenwyck had always said, when life gives you no hope, do what you'd most like to do—then you can die with no regrets.

Closing his hand around a sharp piece of antler, Corwin mentally prepared himself to stab the prince in the belly with it. It wouldn't kill him, but it might surprise him, maybe enough that Corwin could run past him and Faustus and out the door. Assuming the noblemen had arrived without a guard. Corwin thrust his arm upward. . . .

But he was too slow. Vortimer grasped his wrist in a grip like iron and pulled Corwin out from behind the barrels. "Did you think I was so soft, you could kill me with *that?*" cried Vortimer in astonished humor. "The days of the pampered princes vanished with the Romans, silly boy. I've been training to fight since I was three. My father didn't want me to be easy prey like that fool Constans. Now come along like a good fellow and don't make me bruise you too much. My father's wizards want you alive, for the time being."

"Why should I believe you?" Corwin asked, unable to free his wrist from Vortimer's grasp. It was so hard to keep the fear out of his voice and to ignore the constant demands of the mind within his mind saying, *What is happening? What is happening?*

"Why do I care whether you believe me?" Vortimer sneered. "Returning with you will please my father, and I want to keep him pleased, at least until his crown is mine. Now will you come along, or do we have to make mincemeat out of your old friend here first? He was caught harboring a criminal, after all."

Corwin swallowed hard. His stomach felt sick, more from fear than from his mysterious ailment. He was angry at himself for not being able to do something, anything to hurt his captors or escape them. But he didn't want Henwyneb to suffer for his sake like Fenwyck had. "No. I'll come with you if you leave him alone. He doesn't know who I am." Corwin allowed the prince to grab him by the shoulder and pull him to the door.

"Come along, Faustus. We've got what we were sent for."

Faustus looked disappointed. "Do we have to leave so soon?" He put the shell into a pouch at his belt, and Corwin felt a strange sense of pressure around him. It was suddenly harder to breathe.

"The sooner I'm away from this filthy, foul-smelling place, the better," Vortimer growled. He pushed Corwin out the door.

Corwin saw his chance and started to stagger into a run—only to find himself running into the chain-mailed arms of a guardsman, one of two standing next to the horses.

"What have we here, Highness?" asked the guard, grinning. "'Tis a large rabbit you've flushed from its warren."

"It's a thief and a false prophet, not a rabbit," Vortimer grumbled. "Tie him to the back of the horse and let's get going."

"What kind of prophet can't foresee his own capture and avoid it?" asked the other guard.

"As I said, he's a fraud," Vortimer replied.

The forest was so near, and the inner voice was not distracting him at the moment. Corwin decided to bolt for it. He kicked the guard in the knee and tried to push him aside. But as the first guard fell in astonishment, the second guard came up swiftly with his sword drawn. Faustus and Vortimer each grabbed one of Corwin's arms and pulled back tightly.

"It would seem," Vortimer hissed in Corwin's ear, "that your word can't be trusted for anything. But at least now I can truthfully claim that we had to do you harm to prevent you from escaping. You are giving Faustus the opportunity to deliver the thrashing he has been dying to give."

With an ugly smile, Faustus drew back his fist.

"Stop!" cried a high-pitched voice from somewhere down the path.

And everyone did. And stared.

Chapter Four

She was incredibly striking, with long, silvery-blond hair—not the silver of old age, but the shine of newly minted metal. Her eyes were a shade of green-blue that Corwin had never seen before. She was slender, yet muscled, and wore a glimmering but tattered gown of blue and silver fish scales. She didn't look much older than Corwin, but there was strength, determination, and not a little desperation in her eyes. But the strangest thing of all was, when their gazes met, he *knew* her, as if he'd been acquainted with her all his life. He knew that she was from another world vastly different from his own, a world of water, and that she felt very strange upon land. And he knew a dire purpose drove her and had caused her to come seeking . . . him?

He carefully took in every inch of her, and he let out a small gasp as he noticed her hands. He knew those hands—he had seen them during his visions in the forest. He realized that some of those visions must have been her thoughts—that it was she who had mourned over the old drowned merman.

New thoughts struck him—he saw himself, suddenly, from her eyes. *What a skinny, disreputable-looking rat I am!* He felt the other mind within his mind leap with joy at the sight of her, a feeling not unlike Corwin's reactions to the memory of his mother. *What new kind of madness is this? Who is this girl? How does this other mind know her, and why am I caught up in all this? I just wanted to be free and left alone!*

Corwin and the girl's entwined thoughts demanded of each other the same questions: *Who are you? How is this possible?*

Vortimer, Faustus, and the guards were beginning to recover their composure. "Go away, girl!" Prince Vortimer commanded. "This is none of your concern."

She furrowed her brow and didn't budge from where she stood. "Give . . . me . . . the . . . prince," she said, haltingly, as though she were unfamiliar with their language and was still learning it. She was so otherworldly, with such determination in her eyes, that she truly seemed a force to be reckoned with.

Vortimer and Faustus looked at each other. "What do you want with me?" Vortimer asked, an edge of fear to his voice.

Faustus giggled. "Maybe she is the Queen of Fairyland, come to take you off to her bower to be her husband."

"Maybe she is a renegade from some gypsy playacting troupe," suggested one of the guards. "If so, they need a better costumer."

"She doesn't mean *you*," Corwin blurted to Vortimer, somehow knowing this to be true, although the images he was sharing with the strange girl confused him. It had something to do with the shell he had found and the leviathan.

"What? You don't mean to say she thinks *you* are a prince?" Vortimer asked. To the silver-haired girl, Vortimer said, "This boy is only a Prince of Thieves. You're better off without him. Now go, before I lose my good humor."

One of the horses stretched out its neck to get a good whiff of her and she shied back a step.

"It won't hurt you," Corwin said.

"But we will if you don't get out of our way," said one of the guards.

The girl stood her ground and shook her head. She stared at Corwin, her eyes piercing him. "Where is . . . ?" she started to ask, trailing off. In his mind he received the image of the shell again.

She has come to claim the shell. Is that why I'm cursed? Did I steal something I shouldn't have from a princess of the sea? Corwin nodded toward the pouch at Faustus's belt. "He has it."

"I have *what?*" Faustus demanded.

Sighing, Corwin answered, "She wants the shell you took from Henwyneb. He said it wasn't his, remember? Just give it to her and maybe she'll go away."

"In exchange for a kiss, perhaps?" asked Faustus, smirking.

Corwin felt a flash of anger and drove his elbow hard into Faustus's stomach. The nobleman doubled over with a grunt.

"You . . . misbegotten . . . son-of-a . . . ow!" Faustus grunted.

The two guards whipped their swords from their scabbards. "Shall we kill him, Highness?"

"For trying to teach Lord Faustus manners? Alas, no," replied Prince Vortimer. "My father's wizards want the boy alive. They said nothing about damage, however—"

At this, Corwin was flung to the ground, his teeth grinding against the dirt. Faustus kicked him in the back, and Corwin grunted as pain radiated up his side.

"No!" cried the girl.

Corwin felt a hot blast of wind course overhead as if a dragon had unleashed its breath. The horses shrieked. He heard the men around him fall to the ground. Then all was silent.

Corwin dared to glance up. Prince Vortimer, Faustus, and the two guards were splayed on their backs in the dirt, utterly baffled. The horses were rolling their eyes at the girl and straining at their tethered reins. The girl herself was staring at her hands in amazement, as if she couldn't believe what they had done.

"Sorcery," Prince Vortimer hissed as he jumped to his feet, fists clenched and teeth bared like a cornered dog.

Corwin's gut clenched with fear. Only the king was permitted to employ mages—to use magic against the nobility was treason, which was punishable by death. Corwin stared at the girl, trying to convey to her the trouble she was in. "Go!" he cried. "The shell isn't worth your life."

But she didn't leave. "Give me . . . the prince . . . the shell!" she demanded again. "Please . . . it is . . . important!"

Corwin received images that didn't make any sense. A leviathan, but a small one, inside the shell. And this girl called the little leviathan a prince. "Your prince is in the shell?" he asked, bewildered.

"Aha!" said Faustus, snarling with hurt pride and rage. "Somehow you have got the Prince of Darkness himself living in this shell, have you, girl? Is the Evil One the source of your power? Well, you'll not get him back from me. I'll drop him in the nearest font of holy water and banish him back to Hades!"

One of the guards held up his sword by the blade so that it made the sign of the cross. "Begone, witch!" he intoned.

The girl merely tilted her head in puzzlement. "I . . . we . . . need the shell . . . to save my people."

"His Royal Highness, Vortimer, son of King Vortigern and prince of the realm," intoned the other guard, his voice a little shaky, "has commanded you to leave. Do so at once."

The girl gazed at Vortimer with her beautiful aquamarine eyes. "I, too, am of . . . noble family where I come from. My cousin is . . . was . . . going to become a king. But he is dead and . . . my homeland and people are in terrible danger. I might be able . . . to save them. But I must . . . have . . . the shell or I—*we*—," she said, pausing to look at Corwin, "—will die."

Corwin felt his stomach curdle like old milk. *Die? Me? Why? What do I have to do with her people being in danger?*

After a moment's silence, Prince Vortimer started to laugh. "This is the most amazing claptrap I have ever heard. My father has taught me the names of the royal families of every kingdom of importance, particularly princesses, in case a diplomatic match might be made. I have heard of no one who looks like you. Frankly, I don't care if you live or die, sorceress. But I promise you, you will surely die if you stay an instant longer."

The girl sighed heavily and Corwin could feel her frustration and despair, but also her determination and courage. She didn't leave.

If I weren't hurting so much, Corwin thought, *I could take this opportunity to run away. I don't want anything to do with her sorcery or this curse or her prince. I don't want to die. I wish this were all just a bad dream or a hallucination.* But the mind within his mind said, *Stay. Help us. We need you.* As if it *knew* his thoughts.

"Very well," Prince Vortimer said. "I hereby accuse you of using sorcery to attempt harm against the crown of Britain. I sentence you to summary execution. Guardsman, see to it."

The guard holding the sword glanced back at the prince with wide, uncertain eyes. "Y-yes, your Highness." He came at her with his sword upraised. "Kneel, girl, and

I will see that my sword's stroke is swift and painless."

"No, you . . . do not understand!" She held out her arms to deflect him and Corwin saw the palms of her hands. His blood went cold. Her right palm bore the same sun-shaped mark as his did.

Is that a sign of the curse? Did she see the kraken, too? Suddenly Corwin sagged as strength was sapped from his body. Again a great blast of wind flew from the girl's hands and the guards were blown backward. The one with the sword bravely struggled against the flow of air. But his blade began to glow red-hot, and with a cry, he dropped it to the ground.

The inner voice in Corwin's mind was insisting again, *What is happening? What is happening?*

"Peace, my prince," said the girl. "I am trying to . . . free you, so that we may complete . . . the Naming."

She hears it, too! Corwin thought, astonished. *It isn't just in my mind. She called it her prince. So this prince is the one whose thoughts I keep hearing inside of me? But its thoughts seem like those of a little child, not a devil or a royal. And what is a Naming, anyway?*

"Let's get help!" Vortimer said to Faustus. The two noblemen rushed for their horses, untied the frightened beasts, and leaped onto their backs. To the girl, Prince

Vortimer cried, "This attack against the royal family will not go unpunished." To Corwin, he added, "We'll have your head eventually, too, thief. You can count on that!" The pair galloped away, their guardsmen close behind them.

"Ah!" The girl cried out, reaching helplessly after the riders. Corwin realized that Faustus still had the shell.

She raised her hands and Corwin felt even more strength seep out of him. The world seemed to spin and shake around him—these were sensations from the other mind, the prince-mind.

But the girl was now too weak for whatever spell she was attempting and she slumped to her knees on the ground.

Corwin worked hard to force the disorienting feelings from the prince-mind aside. He wanted to get away, to run back to his cave, to pretend this nightmare of a day was finished. But this girl clearly knew more about his mysterious illness. And if he was doomed to die, he wanted to know why. Corwin crawled over to the mysterious sorceress and put a hand on her shoulder. "Are you okay?"

"We have to stop them. We have to rescue the prince," she whispered.

"We?" asked Corwin, hoping she didn't mean him. "Um, I—"

"My prince has marked you. I don't know why. But we will all die if we don't help each other."

"Marked?" Corwin looked at the sun-shaped welt on his palm. *I must have gotten this when I picked up the shell, then.*

"Yes, you now bear the Avatar's mark. The prince's blood is in your blood. That's why we are joined. That's why we will die if we don't complete the Naming."

Corwin gave his head a slight shake. This was all getting too confusing. "Who are you and what's going on?" he demanded. It was bizarre being near her. The other mind found her presence soothing, yearned for her to tell him everything would be all right. Corwin wanted to hear that, too, but suspected that was not what she would tell him.

"Oh. Forgive me," she said, so earnestly that it would have been impossible not to. "My . . . name is Niniane. Of the Bluefin Clan."

Corwin tried to wrap his tongue around the unusual name. "Ninny . . . ninniya . . . what?"

She gave him a wan smile. "Most people just call me Nia."

"Oh. That's easier. Nia. Well, I'm Corwin. And I'm not of any clan."

Nia's face became somber. "I'm sorry to hear that. To be without a clan, without family . . . that's a dreadful thing."

"I hadn't noticed the loss, really." As Corwin said it, he knew it was a lie. Fenwyck had been a poor substitute for the ties of blood and heritage that others had. As if sensing his inner sorrow, Nia put her hand on his shoulder. Corwin couldn't quite make himself shrug it off. "I've done all right. Really. You don't need to pity me. Cousins and brothers and uncles would be just a nuisance to me."

Nia winced and removed her hand. Corwin instantly wished she hadn't. A faint smile appeared again on her face and Corwin realized she could read his thoughts, or at least his feelings. His face flushed hot as he blushed.

Nia looked down at the ground, and Corwin knew she was pretending to ignore his embarrassment. He could also tell she was feeling nearly as ill as he was. *Aha. So I can read her feelings, too. At least we're equal in this.* "Where are you from?" he asked.

"Far away. A place under the sea."

"Are you a merrow, then?"

"What's a merrow?" she asked.

"A mermaid?"

"Mermyd," she corrected him.

"Close enough," Corwin breathed, his eyes wide. He now noticed the delicate, lacy, layered skin on both sides of her neck, which he had thought was part of her gown. *She has gills like a fish!* And her scent was pure salt spray and sea foam, her eyes the color of tide-pool depths. "Um, w-why have you come on land?"

She frowned. "I was . . . beached here. There was a . . . battle . . . in my city. My grand . . . my father . . ."

Corwin received a dizzying array of images of an underwater city, a merman with a knife, an old merman alive and holding a sword, the leviathan from the beach alive and swimming beside him. "Please, slow down. This isn't making any sense."

Nia sighed and nodded in the direction the horses had gone. "Never mind. Now that I'm here, I have to follow the prince and complete the Naming." She looked down at her palm and rubbed at the sun-shaped mark.

"Can you please just tell me, Nia, who is this prince, what is this Naming, and what on earth does this mark mean? I have it, too!" He held out his hand to her.

Nia took his hand in both of hers. Corwin rather liked that and fought down another blush. "Yes, of course," she said. "You bear the prince's mark. He had to give you his . . . fluid, or he would have died. He still may, if we don't find him. And we will die if he does."

"Is that why I'm sick and crazy and hearing thoughts that aren't my own? Has your prince cursed me because I picked up his shell?"

Nia frowned again. "It's not a curse. It's a great honor among my people. You are an Avatar now, or will be if we can complete the Naming. Your mind and the prince's and mine are joined for the rest of our lives. Which may be short, if we can't rescue him."

Corwin felt like kicking a rock in frustration. "Please, please can you explain why I'm doomed to die! I'd like to know what I'm giving up my poor, miserable excuse of a life for. And what prince?"

She gazed at him again with her intense aquamarine eyes. "I'm sorry. There's so much to tell. The prince is the offspring of . . . of . . ." She couldn't seem to find the words, but Corwin received an image in his mind again of the tentacled leviathan alive and swimming. "These beings are from very far away," she said. "*Very* far." She pointed up toward the now darkening sky.

A cool breeze washed over Corwin and he suddenly became aware that, lengthy though summer evenings might be, dusk would be falling soon. And with it might come the kraken.

The door to Henwyneb's cottage opened and the old man shuffled out. "Is everyone all right? What happened?"

Corwin left Nia's side and staggered over to the blind man. "I seem to have escaped royal capture for the moment, Henwyneb."

"I heard a strange battle and the voice of a young girl."

"Yes, yes, I fought them all off. . . . ," Corwin began. He cringed. "Actually, luck was on my side, that's all. Sort of. But we'd better go different ways. I don't want you to get hurt."

Henwyneb waved a hand dismissively. "I'm old. Death will come to me sooner or later in any case. I've little to risk. But who is this girl-witch I heard mentioned?"

"She's amazing, Henwyneb. She says she's a mermaid from under the sea!"

"Really? Where is she? May I meet her?"

"She's here." Corwin guided Henwyneb over to Nia. "Henwyneb, may I present Ninny . . . er, Nia of the Bluefin Clan. Nia, this is Henwyneb, who makes buttons and medicines and very good stew."

Nia stood, wavering a little, and dipped her head. Then she frowned. "He can't see?"

"I've been blind these twenty years," said Henwyneb. "I now see with my fingers. If I may . . . touch your face, lady, then I may know your aspect."

Corwin nodded to reassure her. Nia stepped closer and Henwyneb gently traced his fingers over her face and neck, pausing especially on the feathery gills.

"Astonishing," he whispered. "And where might you be from, good lady of the sea?"

"You won't have heard of it, I'm sure. My home is called Atlantis."

Henwyneb gasped and stepped back.

Corwin blinked in surprise. "Isn't that the place you were telling me about, Henwyneb? The ancient island that sank beneath the sea, in the Roman stories?"

"It is indeed!" said Henwyneb. "But . . . can it be true? The sunken island of myth exists?"

Nia sighed. "Once I would have been . . . chastised for telling you this. We wished to keep our world secret from land-dwellers. Now, perhaps only land-dwellers can save us. But, yes, Atlantis lives. Or did. I don't know how many live there still." She seemed lost in thought for a moment, and Corwin received mental images of blood in water, floating bodies—leviathan and human.

"What happened?" Corwin asked her.

Nia shook her head. "It would take so long to tell you," she murmured, the sadness in her voice overwhelming him. "An evil mermyd . . . wanted power. He killed our kings for it."

"That isn't so unusual," Henwyneb grumbled. "We've got a king like that, too, here on land."

Corwin looked around to make sure the nobles hadn't come back. "Don't let Prince Vortimer hear you say that."

"Bah!" said Henwyneb. "That posturing prince is nowhere nearby . . . is he?" The old button-maker turned his head as if looking around.

"I don't see him, but he may return soon, and with greater forces. We should leave here."

"If the Naming had been completed," Nia said, "I could heal your eyes, ancient one."

"Should that ever come to pass, lady of the sea, feel free to make a return visit. Well, do not let me detain you if you must seek safety. 'Tis a pity you can't stay and tell me your stories, Nia of Atlantis. But bide just a moment more and I will give you cloaks to wear, for I feel the night will be chill."

"I can bear cool weather," said Corwin.

"These cloaks have hoods," Henwyneb added, "so

they may cover any features one might not wish noticed."
He fluttered his hands at his neck.

"Oh." Corwin took note of Nia's lacy neck-gills—not
to mention her silvery hair and shiny gown. She would
hardly be inconspicuous. "Of course. Hoods. Very useful
things, hoods. They keep off bugs, and rain, and suspicion. Good idea, Henwyneb."

The button-maker bustled back into the hovel.

Corwin and Nia looked at each other. The world spun
again a little, as the prince-other-mind fought its own
dizziness. Nia began to sag toward the ground, and
Corwin caught her in his arms. She seemed to draw
strength from him, and he sagged slowly, too, until they
were both kneeling again. "Um . . . I can see you're not
feeling your best right now, but could you tell me just a little more about this prince and why he's doomed us? I
mean, dying just because I found a shell on the beach
seems a little silly, don't you think?"

"The Farworlders," she murmured, and by that Corwin
knew she meant the leviathans. "They're very powerful. The
fluid from one chosen to be prince binds his mind to the mind
of a mermyd. This gives great power to the Avatar—the
mermyd. But first, there must be the Naming. The ritual uses
the power to change the fluid . . . so it's no longer poison."

"So . . . we find the prince, do this ritual, and we're not sick anymore?"

"Yes." She smiled at him. It was a beautiful smile.

However, it wasn't distracting enough to keep one important question from his mind. "But I'm not a mermyd. Will the ritual work for me?"

Nia's smile melted away. "I don't know."

"That's . . . not too encouraging."

"I'm sorry. But we are joined. If the prince dies, we die. If you die, I and the prince die. If I die—"

"I *understand*," Corwin said, a knot forming in his stomach. "I guess you can't make things seem any more dire, can you?"

"We have seven days."

"What?"

"If we don't find the prince in seven days, the poison will kill him."

"And so, us, too."

"Yes. The sunlight is going away. I was marked last night. You had yours—?"

"This morning," said Corwin grimly. "Before dawn."

"So we have—"

"Only six days, really," Corwin finished for her.

"Yes."

The cottage door banged open again and Corwin jumped up, startled. He gently helped Nia stand up.

"Here you are," the old man said, holding out two tattered and patched woolen cloaks.

Corwin took the dark blue one and Nia took the other, a brown one. As Henwyneb had promised, they both had hoods. Corwin put his cloak on, shivering as sunset quickly faded into dusk. He helped Nia with the unfamiliar garment, careful to position the hood so that it completely hid her gills and hair.

He jumped again as a scream rent the air—a scream like a chorus of imps and demons crying out from hell.

"Dear God," Henwyneb whispered. "What is that?"

"The kraken," Corwin answered, his blood turning cold.

Chapter Five

"Is this the serpent from the waves that you saw this morning?" Henwyneb asked.

Corwin nodded and swallowed hard. "Yes," he replied.

"Then you must go, and hurry! Farewell!"

Corwin took Nia's arm. "Get inside, Henwyneb. You don't want to be that snake's supper." Corwin began to walk as fast as his ill and tired body would let him, his hand firmly on Nia's elbow to help her keep up.

But after a few steps, she shook his hand off her arm. "I'm strong enough," she said. "I'm used to dry rooms. I was the best at dry-landing in my school."

"What is a, um . . . never mind. Listen, do you know what the creature that made that scream is?"

Nia stopped. "Show me." She touched his forehead and then her own.

Corwin leaned down and rested his forehead against hers a moment, remembering vividly the scarlet serpent coiling out of the sea, forming huge eyes and a mouth and lunging straight for him.

"I've heard stories of such things," she said at last. "Only the most powerful of Avatars can summon and control the small life of the sea this way. Or an entire council . . ." She paused. "I don't think your blind friend is in danger. I think this thing is only coming for us."

"That's not very comforting," Corwin muttered. "You sure are full of bad news. You didn't have Fenwyck to teach you to only say nice things."

"What is . . . Fenwik?"

"Never mind. That's *my* long story. We should hurry." Corwin was grateful, at least, that the constant disorientation and nagging questioning from the prince-other-mind had quieted down. He couldn't tell if the uneasiness and fear that filled him were entirely his own, or if those feelings also belonged to the Farworlder, or maybe even to Nia. *Fenwyck may have tried to tell me what to think, but he never actually forced his thoughts into my head. If this keeps up, I won't know who I am anymore. And that's almost as good as being dead.*

"Where are we going?" Nia asked as the path connected back to the rutted road.

"We're going to—" Corwin was about to say, "my

cave," but then he realized that the grotto that had shel-
tered him these past several weeks was even closer to the
sea, and therefore now too dangerous a haven. He looked
down the road. The way opposite from the sea headed
straight into Carmarthen town.

Nia studied him, clearly catching his thoughts. "It
may help if we're among others," she said. "It will make
us harder to find."

Corwin racked his brain to try to think of some rela-
tively safe place. All he could think of was the Toad &
Ferret, a rather disreputable tavern with rooms upstairs for
renting. The inn was owned by an old friend, if you could
call him that, of Fenwyck's by the name of Anwir. No one
there was likely to have any love of the royal guards, either.

"I see a place in your mind filled with . . . unpleasant-
looking men who are drinking?"

"You've got it right," Corwin said. "And they don't just
look unpleasant. Most of them *are* unpleasant."

"This place will be safe?" Nia asked, raising her eyebrows in question.

"From the kraken, possibly."

"But . . . there are other dangers?"

"There are always other dangers."

"Yes, I forget I'm among land-dwellers now," Nia said,

sadly staring at the ground. "We were taught about the violence here."

"Well . . . we aren't all bad," Corwin went on, hoping she wouldn't think badly of him just because he was a land-dweller. If they lived long enough, he assumed she would find whole new and unique reasons to think badly of him.

"Raawk!"

Nia jumped back. "Was that the kraken?"

Corwin shook his head. "No, that's just a raven. His name's Nag. And who asked you to comment on land-lubbers, eh?" he called out to the bird. "This is all your fault, you know. You led me to that beached leviathan."

"Does the . . . raven understand your speech?" Nia asked.

"I'm not sure," Corwin said. The bird was regarding Nia curiously, tilting its head one way, then another.

"Is it friendly?"

"No. Ignore him. He only wants to be a nuisance. Let's keep going." As they walked faster down the road, Corwin added, "So why is this serpent creature only after us? What does it want?"

Nia sighed. "Remember I told you about an evil king who wants all power?"

"Yes. You have a Vortigern of the sea."

"In Atlantis, power, magical power, comes from the Farworlders. What you call the leviathan. Our prince may be the last leviathan."

"So this king wants . . . whatever little creature is in that shell?"

"Yes."

"How can there be any power worth having from a baby squid?"

"You've already seen it."

"What, you mean that . . . thing you did with your hands? The blasts of air?"

"Yes. And that's only a small part of it."

Corwin paused. *A small part? Kings and generals would give all their wealth just for the amount of power she'd displayed earlier. Hmm. If I live, is there some way I could profit from all of this?* Corwin could almost see what Fenwyck would have done with Nia. "Behold the Lady of the Sea! Watch her knock over barrels at twenty paces! Only five pence!" But Fenwyck had been a fool, and Corwin was capable of bigger dreams than that.

"I see," Corwin answered carefully.

"If Ma'el can't capture the prince," Nia went on, "he would want to destroy it, so that the prince's power won't interfere with his own. And because we're bound to the prince—"

"Killing either one of us would be as good as killing the prince himself," Corwin finished for her, his body feeling very heavy.

She pressed her lips together. "Yes," she responded.

"And to think, just this morning I was feeling like life couldn't possibly get worse."

"I have felt that way, too," Nia said, the note of sadness back in her voice. "I was wrong."

"Well, we all make mistakes."

"If Ma'el succeeds and destroys the prince, not only will he rule Atlantis, but he will conquer the land-dwelling kingdoms as well. No one will be able to oppose his magic."

Corwin stopped and took Nia by the shoulders. "Nia, maybe we should stop talking about this. I don't really think I can take much more right now."

"I'm sorry," she said. "I thought you wanted to know."

"So did I. I was wrong."

"We all make mistakes," Nia said.

They stumbled on, keeping to the shadows that were growing darker. At least the prince-mind could no longer keep asking, *What is that? What is that?* because nothing could be seen. Corwin hoped they would not be attacked by robbers. Robbers got really upset when their victims had nothing to give. Corwin didn't know if Nia had enough strength to perform more magic, or even how the baby leviathan gave her power. But they were passed by just one lone rider, who gave them only a sidelong glance.

As twilight faded into total night, Corwin and Nia at last came upon a dilapidated building lit by torchlight. The sign hanging above the door showed a badly painted toad and ferret wearing Roman togas. They were either dancing and singing, or walking on hot coals and screaming.

"Are there land-dwellers who look like that?" Nia asked, wide-eyed.

"You'd certainly think so after drinking enough of Anwir's ale," Corwin said.

They went inside, and Corwin was struck by the reek of unwashed men and sour beer. Pulling his hood closer around his face, he guided Nia toward the bar.

"Dija hear that almighty screamin' down by t'beach tonight?" one man was saying behind them.

"Sounded like a horse bein' butchered," said his table partner.

"Probly them bludy Saxons," said the first. "They'll et anythin'."

So others heard the kraken, too, Corwin thought. *Maybe Vortigern will send his wizards to banish it. Although knowing Vortigern, he might just ask his mages to make another kraken for his own uses. So let's hope he doesn't.* At the bar, Corwin noted a stout man bent over, searching for something on low shelves.

"Grown hunchbacked in your old age, Anwir?" Corwin asked.

The man stood up suddenly, banging his head on a shelf above. "Ow! What rascal there be callin' me a hunchback?" He turned around, rubbing his head.

Corwin put a finger to his lips to silence any comment of recognition from Anwir. "Just a friend of a friend."

"Well now, well now," said Anwir, leaning on his side of the bar. "Isn't it nice to have friends?" He smiled at Nia, giving her full view of his stubbly cheeks, nose like a bruised strawberry, and few remaining dark-as-walnut-wood teeth.

Corwin felt Nia's mind beg a question of him, but he couldn't sense about what. "We need a room for the night."

"Of course you do," Anwir said, his gaze not leaving Nia's face.

Unfortunately, Corwin felt it would not be wise to punch Anwir's lights out just now. "Is one available?"

"For a friend of a friend? Always. Assumin' you can pay for it, that is."

Corwin sighed with disgust. *So much for friendship.* And so much for their chances, since he didn't have a penny on him.

Nia tugged at his arm. She was holding a small leather bag. Undoing the drawstrings, Nia spilled out the contents on the bar. There were three pieces of polished coral and five small gleaming pearls. "Will this . . . pay for it?" Nia asked.

Corwin had never seen Anwir's eyes so wide, and he had a feeling his own had grown rather large. If only he'd known Nia had those pearls before! "Why, yes, missy," Anwir said, quickly scooping the gems into his broad, thick palm. "That should just cover it, and a bit left over for breakfast, too." He reached down and got a long iron key from under the counter. "Up the stairs and last door on your right. Have a pleasant evening."

Corwin grabbed the key and guided Nia up the rickety stairs before he could lay a punch on Anwir's smirking face. He also wanted to be out of the common room before anyone took much note of him or Nia. "You shouldn't have given him all the pearls," Corwin grumbled, annoyed.

Nia frowned back at him. "I didn't know how much to pay. I thought he would just take what the room cost and give back the rest. That's what our merchants would do."

"You'll have to be more careful here," Corwin warned. "Not everyone is so honest." *Barely anyone, in fact*, he added to himself. *Including, in another life, me.*

"Land-dwellers," Nia sighed.

The corridor at the top of the stairs wasn't all that inviting. The floorboards tilted at odd angles, and it was lit only with dim, smelly oil lamps in the rusty wall sconces. Corwin walked quickly across the creaking hall to the farthest door on the right. It turned out the key was just a formality, for the lock was broken, hanging uselessly in the hole in the door. Corwin pushed the door open. It was pitch-dark inside.

Suddenly a pale green light gave dim illumination to the room. Corwin looked beside him. Nia stood there with what appeared to be a greenish flame dancing on her hand. But the flame did not burn her skin.

"More of the prince's magic?" Corwin asked.

"Yes," Nia said. "But I don't have the strength to do this for long."

It was enough light, however, for Corwin to see an unlit candle stuck on a block of wood, sitting on a side table. He took the candle and lit the wick on a flame from one of the corridor oil lamps.

So she can create light as well, Corwin thought in amazement. He wondered just how much Nia was capable of doing, or if she even knew. Then a new idea struck him. *Nia's magical power comes from being joined to the prince. But I'm joined to the prince, too. Is it possible that I could have those powers?*

He carried the lit candle back into the room. Its illumination showed a lumpy straw mattress on a bed whose legs were of different lengths. Nia had taken off her cloak and hung it on one of the bedposts. She was standing next to the side table, on which sat a jug of water and a bowl.

Nia poured out some of the water into the bowl and started eagerly splashing her face, neck, and arms with it, letting out happy little noises that made Corwin smile.

What a beautiful creature she is, he thought. *What would she want with a land-dwelling lump like me? Once we find the prince and do that Naming thing, I'm sure she'll want to return to the ocean and leave me behind.*

What am I thinking? He blinked. *This girl and her prince may be the key to my future prosperity, if we live. What nobleman wouldn't pay highly for access to all that power?* But something deep inside of him wondered if he'd ever have the heart to go through with anything like that.

"This water is sweet!" she said.

Corwin found it hard to imagine that the brown swill from Anwir's wells could be called sweet. "Well, it isn't salty like the sea," he said. "It's freshwater, so I guess it doesn't taste like what you're used to."

"Hmmm. Fresh. But empty. It gives no . . . sustenance," she said. "Still, water is water."

"Of course. You need water, don't you? Being a mer . . . I mean, considering where you're from." Corwin didn't know if there was anyone listening at the wall, but it was better to play it safe.

"Is there any more of this?" she asked, pointing at the bowl.

Corwin shook his head. "Anwir would probably charge extra for a bath. And the water wouldn't even be close to warm."

"I don't need warm water," Nia said. "In my home, the water's very cold. Maybe tomorrow . . . is there somewhere nearby where I can swim?"

"The River Twy, maybe, since you don't mind cold water."

"The river, then," she said, and smiled.

His heart nearly melted. And then he remembered she

could sense his thoughts, and he blushed and coughed. To cover his embarrassment, he set the candle down on the table and took off his cloak, draping it over the same bed-post as Nia's. "Um, Nia, I was thinking. If you have . . . abilities because of your . . . connections, does that mean that, well, would I . . . ?"

"Have magic, too?" Nia finished for him. "I don't know. I'm able to speak your language, and it's becoming easier the more time we spend together. I must be learning it from our connection, and from the ocu—from something I have inside of me. But I don't know if there are any rules about this. I've honestly never heard of a Farworlder joined to a land-dweller. But there must have been, once. Before there were mermyds."

"Before?"

"We were created from your kind," Nia explained. "The Farworlders made us to be like them and like you. That's how we share their magic."

Now Corwin really hoped no one was listening. "Then . . . it's possible? That I really could . . . How do you do . . . what you do?"

Nia shrugged. "I think about doing something and then it just . . . happens. Here, I'll show you." She put the candle and its block of wood on the floor and knelt down.

She reached out her arm as if trying to grasp the candle from a distance. Slowly, the block of wood moved, scraping across the floor until it bumped into her hand.

"Let me try," Corwin said eagerly. He lay down on the floor and stretched out his arm. Nothing happened.

"You have to will it to come to you," Nia explained.

Corwin reached out further and concentrated on the candle, insisting, in his thoughts, that it travel to his hand. In a moment, the block of wood bump-bumped over the uneven floor, falling over as it struck a raised plank. Corwin caught the candle before the flame touched the wood.

"You did it!" Nia exclaimed softly.

"I did it," Corwin echoed, amazed. "I did it! Ha! If only old Fenwyck could see me now! What else can I do?"

Nia paused, considering. "Well, Avatars have the powers of moving objects with their minds, expending the energy from their bodies, and sensing the *unis*—which is all of time and fate—which means you can see the possibilities of the near future."

Corwin scowled at the last one. "I already see the future, not that it's ever done me any good. But my visions aren't under my control. And they aren't about me or anyone I know. They certainly never made me and Fenwyck rich. In fact, my master Fenwyck died because of a vision I had in the royal court."

Nia tilted her head, reminding Corwin a little of Nag. "I didn't know land-dwellers had visions," she said.

"I don't think very many land-dwellers do," he said. "It's a pretty rare power, and honestly—I wish I wasn't stuck with it."

"Now that you're joined in your mind to the prince, your control should be better," Nia said.

Corwin was a little nervous about the idea of willfully bringing on a vision. "If I just see more confusing nonsense like usual, how's that going to help us?"

"The prince will guide you," Nia repeated gently but firmly.

"I guess. But it's a little strange having my thoughts mixed up with the thoughts of a baby squid-thing smarter than I am."

Nia smiled encouragingly.

Determined not to let her down, Corwin closed his eyes and thought about the baby leviathan, which must be somewhere in Vortigern's castle by now. All he could sense was darkness and drifting . . . in sweet water. But the prince was weak, lost in sadness.

Help me see what we have to do, Corwin thought.

Dim images of flames and water entered his mind, but that was all. Incalculable sorrow flowed over him . . . homesickness, loneliness, loss, despair. *Come find me. Hurry,* was the only thought Corwin caught clearly from the prince. "He can't help me," Corwin said at last. "He's too weak."

"I know. I sensed it, too."

Corwin felt his strength ebbing away again, and he wondered if the contact with the Farworlder prince had been a mistake. Now all of the despair of the prince was inside of him, making him feel hopeless.

"Tell me something hopeful, Nia," he said. "What other useful spells or powers could we have?"

"We can heal," she said, yawning. "Let me show you." Nia came over and sat down behind him, gently pulling up his shirt.

Her hands felt cool on the skin of his back, and he let himself relax. Then she touched a place on his lower left side and he nearly yelped in pain.

"I thought so," Nia said. "Your skin is all purple here. Like a stain of squid ink."

"Where Lord Faustus kicked me," Corwin groaned. "It must be bruised pretty badly. I'm surprised he didn't break a rib."

"Let me heal you," Nia said. Suddenly warmth spread from the palms of her hands into the skin and muscles of his lower back. His pain was eased, and he could feel the sinews regaining their health. "Ah, that's wonderful. Thank—"

Nia slumped against his back, her head falling between his shoulders.

"Nia? Nia?" Corwin turned around and caught her as she slipped toward the floor.

"Tired now," Nia whispered. "Sleep . . ."

Healing me must have really drained her, Corwin thought, wincing in guilt. He stood and took her in his arms, then carried her to the bed, placed her on the straw mattress, and covered her with his cloak.

Though the sorrow from the prince-squidling was still in him, Corwin also felt a wild, triumphant hope. *If I have magical powers, true magic, I could outshine Fenwyck! No need for tricks and Hammurabia and sleight of hand. No need to sell Nia. Kings will give bags of gold to me as I mow down enemy armies for them, and heal the royal children, and make predictions for the kingdom. Yes, the future may be very bright indeed.*

If he lived to see it, of course.

Taking the other cloak as a blanket, Corwin blew out

the candle and curled up on the floor. "No worse than sleeping in the cave," he muttered and soon fell fast asleep.

Corwin's eyes blinked open, and he gazed around the dingy room, struggling to remember where he was. He had had very bizarre dreams. Dreams of swimming in cold, dark water, a beautiful, glimmering city beneath him. Dreams of being curled up tight and warm, lazily feeding himself scraps of seaweed or fish with his tentacles.

Corwin focused more clearly on his surroundings. *I shouldn't be here*, he thought. But somehow he wasn't sure if the thought was his or someone else's. And then it all came back to him—why he was here and who he was here with.

Corwin rolled over and looked at the bed. Nia was still there, still asleep. He got up and went to the window, squinting at the beams of sunlight slanting in. He pushed one of the shutters slightly open. Birds chirped and horses whickered in the clearing below. It was midmorning. And he had only five days left to live.

"Nia, Nia!" Corwin shook her shoulder. "Wake up."

"Mmm?" She made movements as though trying to swim and then began to gasp, her gills working in and out like bellows.

"Nia, are you all right?"

"So heavy . . . must get to water . . . uuuhhh," she groaned and writhed.

Corwin ran to the side table, grabbed the bowl, and threw the tepid standing water onto her.

She sat upright, trying to catch the water running down her hair and face, and he tried to direct the water to her gills. The gills seemed to drink in the liquid, but Nia coughed and sputtered.

Corwin threw down the bowl and sat beside her. "Is there anything I can do?"

Gasping, Nia said, "I dreamed I was trapped in a dry room. Now I'm awake, but it's just like my dream."

Corwin was beginning to get an idea of what a dry room might be. For someone who had lived her life in water, it had to be horrible. "We have to get you to the river so you can swim."

"Yes. Swim. In the river."

Corwin picked up her cloak and threw it over her shoulders, putting the hood up over her silvery hair. Even though it was quite warm, he put on his own cloak as well, disguise being more important right now than comfort. "Breakfast will have to wait," he said. "We don't want to stay here any longer than we have to. Word may have gotten back to the castle already of where we are. Given what Anwir usually serves for breakfast, we won't be missing much."

He helped Nia get out of bed and stand up. A nagging feeling in the back of his mind became a voice. *You are awake. What is happening? What is happening?*

Corwin and Nia both sighed at once. "We're coming to find you, er, Highness," Corwin said, not knowing if the title was appropriate.

Nia smiled a little. "As he said, my prince, we will find you."

Good. I tried to heal you during your sleep. You will not be as sick for a while. But I am very weak now. Come find me. Hurry.

Corwin realized he did feel a little better, though he still would rather have curled up in a corner and slept for three days. He knew it made sense since Nia had picked up his language, but he was still a little disturbed to find that the baby-prince-squid-thing had learned the tongue so quickly. Nia was his age, but the prince was so young!

Your thoughts, sent the prince, *are mine now.*

That was even more disturbing.

Nia's cool hand closed on his arm. "It's for the best. You'll see."

"I hope so," Corwin said, "because five days from now I may not be seeing anything."

He helped Nia get her balance, and they went out the door and into the hallway. All seemed quiet, normal for a tavern in the morning. He hoped. He guided her down the stairs. The common room was empty except for one man with his head down on a table loudly snoring.

"Hmm, Anwir's being charitable," Corwin murmured. "Usually he throws everyone out at dawn. I bet he'll charge this man a night's room rent when he wakes up." There was a basket of rolls on the table. Corwin snatched three of them and put them in a pocket of his cloak. *If nothing else*, he thought, *they might be useful as weapons, given how hard they are.*

As Corwin looked around, he felt a chill pass down his spine. There was something unsettling about the stillness in the inn. "I don't think we should leave that way," he blurted out just as Nia reached the front door.

"Should we go through one of these?" Nia asked, pointing at a window, as if it were a completely sensible question.

"Um, no, I think that would be worse, for being noticed, than the front door. C'mon. Anwir must have a secret back door to this place, considering the kind of men who come here." As he led Nia past the bar into the kitchen, Corwin took one look back at the common room. For a moment he thought the sleeping man's eyes might be slightly open, watching him. But Corwin couldn't be sure, and he didn't have time to worry about it now.

Chapter Six

They found a secret way out through the back of a narrow pantry beside the inn's kitchen hearth. Both Corwin and Nia were coated in a light dusting of ashes by the time they came out.

"What's this powder?" Nia asked, trying to wipe it off but only smearing it worse on her hands and face.

"It's soot," Corwin replied. "You'd better just leave it on. It'll help with our disguise."

As luck, or Anwir's design, would have it, the bushes behind the inn came right up to the secret back door, so they were able to duck out among the trees without being noticed.

Normally, a walk to Carmarthen Castle would take only a couple of hours or so from the Toad & Ferret. But that meant going through the center of Carmarthen town, which Corwin was not willing to risk in daylight.

So they skirted the town, keeping to the wooded areas surrounding the farm fields, ducking low whenever another person seemed near. This took much longer.

"If you don't mind," Nia gasped after they had been wandering for about two hours, "is the river near? I really have to swim."

Corwin sighed, glancing at the tall trees surrounding them. "I—I'm not sure where the river is at the moment," he said. *We aren't lost*, he told himself. *We can't be lost. Dear God, tell me we aren't lost. Oh God, we're lost.*

"Rawwwk!" came Nag's cry from the branches overhead.

"Oh, that's just like you," Corwin growled at the bird. "You always show up at a good time to laugh at me." Corwin took one of the rolls out of his cloak pouch and threw it at Nag. The raven jumped up and deftly caught the bread roll in his talons, then flew off through the trees to their left.

"Miserable clever bird," Corwin muttered. "You tricked me into giving you some of our breakfast. Not that I wanted to break a tooth on Anwir's baking. Maybe your beak will break and that will be punishment enough!"

"Rawk rawk rawk rawk," Nag called from a distance. It really did sound like laughter. And then came a splash.

Nia peered around a tree toward Nag's noises. "Corwin, look! Your bird found water!"

"What?" Corwin stood beside Nia and looked. Just a

few yards away, Nag was happily swooping up, then dropping the roll into . . . a small lake. Nag picked up the floating roll, flew up, then dropped it again, with another splash. The bird picked it up one more time, then dropped it onto the lakeshore with a thunk, alighted beside it, and began to nibble away at the now soggy roll.

"All right, so he's smarter than he seems. He's still a nuisance."

But Nia had already left Corwin's side. She ran up to the lake, threw off her cloak, and waded in. Corwin hurried to catch up to her.

He paused on the lakeshore. There was something a bit eerie about the place. A light mist rose from the water, particularly around the edge of the lake. The sunlight seemed to dim, even though there were no clouds in the sky. It felt like the very trees were paying attention to them. There was a sense of importance about the lake. Corwin felt a bit of the sorrow he had felt the previous day returning. He didn't like seeing Nia swim in this water. There was something wrong and he didn't know what, which he found very annoying. *Is this more of the Farworlder prince's poisoning?* he wondered.

You sense the unis, the prince's "voice" said in his mind. *Fate is heavy in this place.*

What will happen here? Corwin asked.

I cannot see. I am too weak. It is too far from now.

Then I will make sure to avoid this place in the future, Corwin thought. *Assuming I live to have a future.* "Nia!" he called out. "You should come out of there as soon as you can."

Nia swam closer to where he stood on the lakeshore. "Why? Corwin, you should come in. This water's very healthful."

"No, thank you. I don't like the slimy moss that grows on lake bottoms. But listen, there's something strange about this place. Even your prince thinks so. Can't you feel it?"

Nia stood up in the shallows and looked around. "No. I don't feel anything. It's very peaceful here. I wish I could stay."

"Well, we can't. We have to get to your prince, remember?"

Nia smiled. "I'm glad you now see our goals as one. Just let me swim a little bit more." She turned and slid under the surface, her long hair streaking like wet lightning as she swam.

Corwin sat down on the lakeshore feeling miserable, itching to leave. He took another roll from his cloak pouch and dunked it in the lake water, letting it soak for a while. Then he picked it up again and took a big bite, gagging almost instantly. It tasted like stale bread and pond scum.

He managed to get down one swallow and then threw the rest at Nag. "How can you stand this stuff?" Then the prince-mind within said, *Ah, that was very good. I wish I had some.* To Corwin's shock, his hand reached out and picked up the roll again. He continued to eat it, one part of his mind loathing it, one part enjoying it thoroughly. It was just as Nia had said—slowly, his goals were melding with those of Nia and the prince. *If this is being "joined," then maybe death wouldn't be such a problem.*

"Don't be silly," Nia chided as she emerged from the lake. There was something regal in the way she carried herself that made it easy for Corwin to believe she had been among the royalty where she came from. "In time, you and the prince will be as one. He'll enjoy what you enjoy, and you'll enjoy his delights as well. It's nothing to be afraid of."

"I hope you're right," Corwin said, with a halfhearted smile. *Though I doubt it*, he couldn't help thinking.

Nia tousled his hair as she passed him. Corwin jerked back his head, annoyed. But he wouldn't have minded so much if she did it again sometime.

They continued to follow deer paths through the woods, and finally Corwin was able to glimpse the tops of the towers of Carmarthen Castle far off in the distance. *So, we aren't lost after all. Just running out of time.*

But Corwin perhaps had his gaze too firmly on the goal, for just then he tripped and fell flat on his face. "Ooof!"

"Are you all right?" Nia asked.

"I'm fine," Corwin muttered, embarrassed. He turned to see what root or fallen branch had tripped him up. But it was a rock . . . a rock with inscriptions on it. Curiosity got the better of him and he looked closer. "Probably some old Roman ruin." But the letters weren't Latin— Fenwyck had taught him to read that language a little, so he could at least recognize the amount on Roman coins or tell which documents were valuable enough to be worth stealing.

But Nia gasped and crouched down beside the stone. "I know this—it's the language of my people!"

Corwin's eyebrows shot up. "So what's it doing here?" he asked.

"I have no idea." Nia lightly dusted the stone with her fingers. "Shrine of the . . . The rest is broken off. These are symbols for earth and water," she said, pointing to the etchings.

"Could it have washed ashore a long time ago, from your city?" Corwin felt stupid as he asked it. He knew that stones rarely came up from the sea depths to shore. "Or maybe it fell off a ship?"

"My people don't use ships," Nia replied. She stood and looked around. There was an overgrown hill to the west. Nia crept through the underbrush toward it.

"Nia? Nia, what are you doing? We don't have time for any side trips, Nia, remember?"

"But this is important! I can feel it. I just want to look . . . oooah!" she shrieked and disappeared.

"Nia!" Corwin ran toward where she had been and suddenly slid down into a slanting hole. He skittered and bumped and landed right beside her on a stone platform. There were stairs ahead of them leading down into darkness.

"Oh, Nia," Corwin sighed as the unis feeling of foreboding closed over him again. "We *really* shouldn't be here."

"But what is this place?" Nia asked. "Why haven't I heard about these shrines in land-dweller kingdoms?"

"Why are you asking *me*? Do I look like a keeper of

Atlantean knowledge? You should ask your prince." Corwin slowly got up and dusted himself off.

Nia closed her eyes a moment. "He doesn't know, either. But he senses its importance within the unis." She ran her fingers over the inscriptions and images on the wall—images of octopuses and mermyds and dolphins.

Corwin could feel homesickness radiating from her. He gently grasped her upper arm. "Nia, come on. I know all this reminds you of your homeland, but if we stay here much longer, you won't live to see it again."

"You're right," Nia said, determination returning to her face. "I lost sight of my purpose for a minute. It's good that you're here with me. The prince chose his land Avatar wisely."

Chose wisely? Corwin thought as they began to crawl back out of the hole. *And here I thought I was just in the wrong place at the wrong time.*

It took a little while for Corwin to catch sight of the castle again. But once he had, the path opened wider and wider until it led onto a clearing surrounded by trees. Castle Carmarthen was not far away, just over a slight rise.

"Looks like we finally got some luck," Corwin murmured.

"Corwin," Nia warned.

Suddenly the bushes ringing them shifted and rustled. Armed and liveried men on horseback emerged from under the trees into the clearing. "Guess again," Anwir said, riding on a stout pony. "Luck is with someone today, but not you. There they are, your lordship," Anwir told a rider who had the armor and tabard of the captain of the guard.

Corwin prepared to grab Nia and run, but the rest of the horsemen closed around them in a semicircle. "Just when I was sure I couldn't possibly think any worse of you, Anwir, you've gone and proven me wrong," Corwin said.

The insult didn't seem to bother Anwir a bit. Instead, he responded with a broad grin. "Why, thank ye, lad. I've your late master's reputation to surpass, ye know."

"Oh, you've well surpassed Fenwyck in villainy, Anwir." Corwin turned round and round, looking for a hole in the circle, some avenue of escape. But there was none. "How did you find us?"

"My man followed you," Anwir said, pointing at a bush. From behind it emerged the man who had been "sleeping" at the inn table. "He said you made enough noise crashing through the woods that a deaf man could have tracked you."

Corwin sighed. *Fenwyck always said I was too clumsy to be a good house-thief.* Continuing to study the circle of riders, Corwin recognized one of them—one of the mages from Vortigern's court. The mage leaned over and whispered in the captain's ear. The captain nodded. "Enough of this chatter," he declared. "Corwin of Carmarthen, you and your sorceress companion are under arrest for assault upon a royal personage. You are to accompany us to the court of His Royal Majesty, King Vortigern, where you will be tried and sentenced for your crime."

All the riders looked wary and had their hands on sword hilts or bows. The mage looked as though he had a spell gesture prepared to unleash.

But Corwin knew their preparation was unnecessary. Even if he and Nia had had the strength of last evening, they could not have overcome so many. Weak as they were today, it was hopeless. "I'm sorry," he whispered to her. "I failed you."

To his surprise, she shook her head. "These people will take us into the castle, won't they?"

"Probably."

"Then we will be closer to our prince. We haven't failed yet."

Yesterday she was the voice of doom; today she is the

voice of insane hope, he thought. *I'm not sure which voice I like less.*

Corwin allowed the guards to escort him and Nia to a wooden wagon on which sat a large wicker cage. The guards motioned for them to get into the cage, which Corwin and Nia reluctantly did. Corwin tried to reach out mentally to the Farworlder prince. *What do we do now?*

I cannot help you. Come find me. Hurry.

Big help you are, Corwin thought and then immediately chided himself. The prince *had* done all he could to help. What more could one expect from a baby squid-thing? Corwin felt his gut clench at the thought of again meeting the king who killed Fenwyck. *If we live, and I keep my magical power, maybe I'll have the chance to teach Vortigern a lesson.* It seemed like just another insane hope, but it gave Corwin strength.

Anwir cleared his throat. "Now as to that reward, my good fellow . . . ," he began, addressing the captain.

"You will be paid when the king is assured that these are the criminals he wished apprehended," the captain replied.

"But . . . but . . . didn't your wizard there just confirm that for you?"

"As I have said, the king himself must decide. Now be

off to your business, man, and let us be about ours." He rode away, leaving Anwir sputtering.

Corwin smiled sourly. *There's no honor among thieves, Anwir. You probably won't see a penny for betraying me.*

The driver at the front of the wagon shouted to the horses, and the wagon jerked forward with great jolts and bumps. The ride was going to be anything but comfortable.

"What is this King Vortigern like?" Nia asked.

"A nasty piece of work, really," Corwin answered. "He doesn't trust anyone, he's afraid of everything. We definitely can't expect justice or mercy from him." Corwin noticed the guard riding closest to the wagon scowling at him. *So I'm speaking treason. So what? I'm dead already. I can't make anything worse than it is.* "In fact," Corwin went on, "people say he stole the crown by killing the king before him and that king's son. And that he gave land to Saxon mercenaries in exchange for one of their women as a wife. And that he's a heretic—"

"That's enough!" roared the guardsman, drawing his sword. "You will speak no more treason, varlet, or I will cut your tongue out."

"I'm only saying what everyone already knows."

"You are spreading vile gossip invented by the king's enemies."

"Hmm. Hoping for a promotion in the ranks, are you?"

As the sword was thrust through the wicker bars, Corwin leapt back, protecting Nia. "All right! All right!"

The mage in the scarlet robe rode back to see what the commotion was and had a soft word with the angry guardsman. The guardsman calmed down a little and sheathed his sword, but the scowl never left his face.

"You aren't allowed to talk about your king?" Nia asked.

Corwin shook his hand. "Kings are considered more than men here," he explained. "The only person more powerful than a king is the pope."

"What's a pope?"

Corwin tried not to let his eyes bulge. It was so strange to meet someone who didn't know these things. "He's the leader of the Catholic Church," he said.

"What's the Catholic Church?"

"Uh-oh—you'd better not say that in front of the king," Corwin warned. "It's . . . hard to explain. Tell me about who holds power in your country."

"In my city we had ten kings," Nia said. "Farworlders, each joined to a mermyd Avatar, the way you and I are joined to the prince. They ruled together in the High and Low Councils and used their magical power to run the city and heal people." She paused, her eyes clouding over. "But I don't know if any of them survived," she added in a softer tone. She raised her gaze slightly to meet his. "Do you think King Vortigern will kill us?"

Corwin's jaw tightened. "If we're lucky," he said. "But given the way kings are, especially ones like Vortigern, he might want to try some torture first. Boiling oil, or maybe a bed of spikes. Just to make his point."

Nia sighed. "Land-dwellers."

Now would have been a wonderful time, Corwin thought, to be struck with a vision of an old Corwin, gray-bearded, playing with grandchildren. But no such vision came.

They rode the rest of the way to Carmarthen Castle in silence.

Chapter Seven

As the wagon bumped over the drawbridge, Corwin glanced up at the crenellated wall. The iron cage in which Fenwyck had been exposed was still there. And from the looks of the skeletal arm that draped over the side, so was Fenwyck. Corwin shivered.

"What are you looking at?" Nia asked.

"My old guardian, Fenwyck. Or what's left of him. A man who was like a father to me. But Vortigern had him killed."

"Oh." A wave of sympathetic feeling came from Nia. "I had a similar loss—also because of an evil king."

Again Corwin saw in his mind the gray-haired merman lying on the sand. Corwin reached over to grasp Nia's hand. Together, for some moments, they shared their sorrow.

The wagon stopped with a sudden jolt. A guardsman came around to open the back of the wicker cage. "Come out!" he commanded.

Corwin and Nia crawled to the back of the wagon and were hoisted out by the none-too-gentle guards. They were taken without ceremony into an antechamber and soon thereafter marched into the presence of the king.

The throne room now looked very much like a throne room, Corwin noticed. All the rugs, tapestries, and side tables were in place. Corwin saw that one side table still had a dent in the leg from where he'd kicked it over weeks ago, and he smiled. The two-stepped dais was in place, with two high-backed thrones on it. One throne was occupied by an uncomfortable-looking young woman whom Corwin assumed was the Saxon girl Roxanna. The other held His Majesty, King Vortigern, in stiff purple robes, looking decidedly less casual than he had the first time Corwin had met him.

All three mages stood beside the dais, huddled together and watching Corwin and Nia intently. Beside them stood Prince Vortimer, arms folded across his chest, his mouth set in a gloating smirk.

The guards forced Corwin and Nia to their knees before the thrones. "Majesty, we bring before you the two criminals who attacked your son."

"Well, well, well," Vortigern said, staring at Corwin. "If it isn't the young prognosticator and lackey to a clumsy thief. I'll have you know, fellow, that I had the viaducts below the castle searched, and there are no fighting dragons there. You must have been mistaken."

"As I told Your Majesty," Corwin said, "the visions may have had nothing to do with you. You had no reason to be angry."

The guard beside Corwin cuffed him on the ear.

"Who gave you permission to speak? A king's wrath is always justified, let that not be forgotten." Vortigern turned his attention to Nia. "And what is this bizarre creature whom you have selected to join you in your life of crime?"

Nia tried to stand but the guard beside her kept her down with a hand on her shoulder. "Your Majesty," she cried, "I am Niniane of the Bluefin Clan, last Avatar of the ancient kingdom of Atlantis."

At this the throne room erupted in a hubbub, and the three mages stared and whispered to one another. The king held up his hand and the noise in the room subsided. With a disbelieving raise of the eyebrows, Vortigern said, "Go on."

"I beseech you to help us. I meant no harm to your son. But his companion had taken a shell that contains the last prince of Atlantis, and I had to rescue the prince—"

At this, the king burst out laughing. "You have a prince . . . in a shell? Tiny like a fairy, is he? Curled up like a little pearl in an oyster?"

"If you please!" Nia cried. "If I could have the shell, I could show you."

Vortigern looked at his son, Vortimer. "Is there a shell?"

"Indeed. A pretty thing that we took as a tithe from an old button-maker. Faustus had it last."

"Go and fetch it hither."

With an annoyed rolling of the eyes, Vortimer left the throne room.

"Thank you, Majesty," Nia said. "That is wise. For what destroyed my city may come to conquer your kingdom, too."

Vortigern's visage immediately lost its mirth. He leaned forward on his throne, resting one elbow on his knee. "What is this danger you speak of?"

"We had a king who was banished from the High Council," Nia began, her voice clear and her speech smooth. "His name is Ma'el. But he didn't accept his banishment, and he has tried to seize more power by killing all of the High and Low Councils. He can take sorcerous power from the kings he has killed, and by now he is the most powerful Avatar that Atlantis has ever seen. But he also wants to rule the land-dwelling kingdoms. Once his control of Atlantis is complete, he will one by one destroy all the land kingdoms until he rules the entire world. I beg you, let us be in alliance together against him, so that I may have some chance to save my people and yours."

A deep silence filled the throne room. Corwin did not like what he saw on Vortigern's face. Fear, suspicion, and anger were warring behind the king's eyes. At last, Vortigern said, "Who sent you, girl?"

"Sent me? No one . . . I came here . . . your guards brought me. . . ."

Corwin was momentarily distracted as the prince-voice in his mind cried, *What is happening? What is happening?* Corwin felt as though he were being lifted up and carried. *Ah. Vortimer must have found our prince. Relax, little one. You're being brought to us.*

I am afraid, the prince responded.

"Do not act the innocent, child," King Vortigern was saying, as he stood and walked down the dais toward Nia. "I have many enemies. Any one of whom would love to have a spy in my court, and to see me quaking in my boots over some supernatural threat to the throne. I seem to have gotten a reputation as one who will believe any sort of superstitious nonsense. Well." He leaned down toward her. "I don't believe *you*, or your ridiculous story about Atlantis!"

As Nia gasped in dismay, Prince Vortimer pressed through the crowd to his father's side. "Here's the shell, Father. Faustus had tossed it into the baptismal font in the mistaken belief that the Devil resided in it. The priests were all too happy to have me fish it out again for them."

"The Devil, you say? Well, let's just see what's in here, shall we?" Vortigern jammed two fingers down into the hole of the shell.

Corwin felt as though a blow had landed across his arms and stomach. He felt the little Farworlder's pain and fear and knew the prince would try to defend himself.

"Ow!" Suddenly King Vortigern jerked his hand out again. "Something *bit* me!"

Corwin could almost taste the king's blood in his mouth. *Good for you, little squid!* he couldn't help thinking. *You showed him. I wish I could bite him, too.*

The courtiers gasped. "Forgive him, Majesty," Nia jumped in. "My prince meant no harm, but you scared and hurt him."

Vortigern glared at Nia. "What kind of trick is this? Did you hope to poison me?"

"No, no!"

He gave the shell back to Vortimer. "Put it back in water, but make sure it's boiling water this time. Perhaps we'll serve it up in the evening's soup."

"NO!" Nia had to be restrained by the guard holding her.

Corwin reached out his arm toward Vortimer as he had to the candle back at the inn. He concentrated on summoning the shell to his hand. But he only succeeded in making him drop the shell once. Vortimer was able to pick up the shell and leave with it without Corwin accomplishing anything other than draining both himself and Nia of strength.

"You fool!" Nia shouted at King Vortigern, tears running down her face.

"What did you call me?!" King Vortigern roared back at her.

"You fool! What have you done? You're destroying my people! You will destroy yours as well!"

"Enough of your insolence!" Vortigern slapped Nia across the face. "You are a spy and hereby sentenced to death!"

"No!" Corwin cried. He lunged forward to somehow protect Nia. But he was tackled by two guards and held to the floor. Because he had expended so much strength trying to retrieve the shell, Corwin could only struggle in vain.

As the guards picked up an angry, glaring Nia, Vortigern commanded, "Put her in the iron cage on the wall. She can entertain the people below with her amusing pleas for help."

"You will regret this!" Nia cried as she was carried out of the throne room. "Corwin, you must save the prince!" was the last thing she said before the door closed behind her and the guard.

Corwin slumped to the floor in despair. *Again I'm the cause of someone else's death, and in the same way. And Nia is far more innocent than Fenwyck.* Images and strange words flooded his mind for a moment. *This is the Naming.* Nia was trying to teach him the healing ritual, in case he should have a chance to rescue the Farworlder prince. *You are a brave girl*, he tried to send back to her, *but it's probably hopeless.*

Other impressions came to him. The prince's shell had been dropped in water again. Corwin could feel how the Farworlder's skin was being soothed, and he could breathe easily again. The water was tepid warm, but not hot, not yet. There were other sea creatures, mussels and clams and crab, near him, most of them dead. The water tasted of their decaying flesh. . . . A pair of soft leather boots appeared at Corwin's eye level, beneath the hem of a purple robe. "Now as for you——," King Vortigern began.

"Please, Majesty," Corwin said, trying desperately to think of some trick, some lie, some deal he could offer that would make the king release Nia. Telling Vortigern of his magical powers would do no good now—Corwin had expended all his sorcerous strength. He wouldn't be able to prove it. All he could say, at last, was, "Punish me. I brought Nia here. The girl is innocent. Put me in the cage, not her." Then Corwin realized his stupidity. *If I die, she dies anyway. What kind of a rescue is that?* And since when was he so valiant? But deep inside of him, there were new feelings—feelings he'd never experienced before. And he knew that he would be willing to give his life for Nia's, if it were actually possible.

"How very sweet," King Vortigern said. "But I don't take kindly to threats and insults, as you must have noticed. However, I don't expect she will die right away, a healthy young thing like that. There may still be time to change my mind, if I'm given reason to."

Change his mind? Then there's a chance! But what is it he wants? Corwin wondered. "What . . . sort of reason might that be, Majesty?"

"You call yourself a seer. Perhaps you can . . . foretell what reason may sway me." The king stretched and yawned. "I feel like taking a bit of fresh air in the courtyard. Let those who would enjoy my company come with me." Vortigern walked away. In fact, the whole throne room emptied, as all courtiers wished to be in the company of the king. All departed, except the guard, who was nearly sitting on Corwin, and the three mages.

The blue-robed mage, whose name was Anguis, approached him. "Will you promise not to harm us and not to flee if we send your guard away? It is in your interest, and that of your friend, if you so promise."

Fenwyck had taught Corwin that promises were merely ways to make other people do what you wanted, and a way to buy time for yourself. Corwin decided, however, that the stakes were too high this time to lie. "Yes, I swear."

Anguis nodded at the guard and Corwin felt a great weight come off his back. As the guard walked away, Corwin sat up. For a moment he was tempted to jump up and head for the door. But he did not want to buy his freedom again with someone's life. And it would hardly matter—as soon as Nia or the Farworlder prince died, he'd die, too. Therefore, he stayed.

"We have convinced His Majesty to give you this chance," Anguis said, "because we feel you have genuine talent. On the night before your last visit here, we cast oil upon the water and read the scapulae, and received an oracle similar to the vision you described. However, we"—Anguis looked back at Red Robe and Leather Cap—"know our king's moods and chose not to speak of our visions. We put forth great effort to find you, hoping that enemies of the king would not find you first."

Corwin paused at this new turn of events. *It seems I might have a card worth playing after all.* "But His Majesty disapproved of my vision."

"His Majesty is of a nature to misread things in light of his fears."

"How might I prevent his displeasure again?" Corwin asked carefully.

"By giving His Majesty what he wants."

Corwin stifled his impatience. "And what might that be?"

Anguis sighed. "We're trying to tell you, boy. Speak to the very things he fears. As you have heard from the king's own mouth, he has enemies who wish to take the crown from him. They believe he won the throne unfairly, that he isn't the rightful king."

Corwin kept his mouth shut, lest he blurt out that he believed that, too.

"His Majesty would like to know," Anguis went on, "who these enemies are, preferably *before* they have the chance to strike and do harm. If you have the ability to identify who is likely to lead such a rebellion, His Majesty would find this information . . . very useful."

Corwin's heart fell as he realized the trap he was being led into. *If I name someone, anyone, as a rebel, that person will die. So I can only buy Nia's life with that of someone else. I could name someone vile, like Anwir. But then I'd be sinking even lower than him. And what if the king wants more names? How many would I doom with words just to save my own skin and my friend's? No, even I can't stoop to this.* "I . . . can't see the future like that," Corwin tried to explain. "I can't choose what to see. The visions just happen. And I almost never see a person's features or hear a name."

Anguis pursed his lips. "Nonetheless, if you tell us the details of your visions, perhaps we may be able to divine the meaning of the symbols. For example, we believe the bear that you saw charging across the ocean to be the brother of the late former king, Uther Pendragon. We may be able to read what you, who are untrained, cannot."

So you get to choose who dies, Corwin thought. *I don't think that's much of an improvement*. Something else occurred to him. "Wasn't there something in your vision about the tower that included a sacrifice?" he asked. "I remember Prince Vortimer mentioning that."

Anguis flushed in embarrassment, then cleared his throat. "Well. I must ask you to speak nothing of what I am about to say to the king, or anyone else. The tower he is building is on unstable ground. Beneath this castle are labyrinths of catacombs and waterways that served the Roman fortresses. Many of these are collapsing from lack of repair, and the additional weight of the tower is only making matters worse.

"But you've seen how His Majesty deals with set-backs. He doesn't believe his architects, and therefore he consulted us. We had to give him some sort of supernatural reason, and therefore a supernatural cure."

Leather Cap spoke up. "Water nixies. I'm telling you, we should have kept to the water-sprite theory."

Anguis sighed and rolled his eyes. "Then Vortigern would have had us hunting the river for sprites. And if we couldn't produce one, what would have happened to us?" To Corwin he added, "It's too bad you didn't bring that girl to *us* first. She looks a little like a water nixie should look. We might have been able to pass her off as one."

Corwin narrowed his eyes, realizing just how low these men were. "So instead you thought a boy with no father to defend him wouldn't be missed," he said, "and could be sacrificed with no problem."

Anguis bristled. "We didn't think His Majesty would bother to go to the trouble of finding the child. We assumed that the outcry from his other counselors would stop him."

Leather Cap shook his head and clicked his tongue. "Never underestimate the pigheadedness of His Majesty."

"Shhh!" Red Robe hissed, glancing around them.

Never underestimate the horrible things men can do in order to save themselves, Corwin thought. He tried not to consider the fact that he had been in that category himself not too long ago.

"Actually, you wise men should be talking to the girl, Nia," Corwin said. "She's much cleverer and more skilled in magic and visions than I am. And she really is from the city of Atlantis. Her people have knowledge far beyond what we know, but they need our help. You could learn a lot from Nia."

The three mages all chuckled. "Dear boy, Atlantis is a *myth*," Red Robe said. "A fable, invented by the Romans.

Oh, maybe once there was a cataclysm that sank an island in the Mediterranean Sea. But I myself have been to that sea, and there are many islands bearing volcanoes, which now and then explode with great force. A myth of an island sunk by divine powers is bound to arise. Myths of ancient wisdom are natural, for were the Greeks not wiser than we?"

Leather Cap spoke then. "Your friend is an albino, lad. I have seen such people with pale hair and striking features. Perhaps she came up with the Atlantis story so that others wouldn't think she was some kind of monster. It adds some glamour to her strangeness."

Corwin shook his head. "That can't be, magus. She and I can share thoughts, visions. She has shown me what her world is like." Some instinct kept him from saying more about the prince in the shell.

"You seem ill, lad," Anguis said. "Could she have fed you anything or drugged you in some way? You know, there are tinctures that make a man susceptible to believing whatever he's told. She could have guided your thoughts with words until you saw precisely what she wanted you to see."

Corwin blinked, then looked down at the ground. *I was poisoned; she even told me so*, he thought. *And I've never actually seen the creature in the shell. She only told me that the voice I'm hearing is coming from the prince. What if she's the one who brought the kraken . . . no, it was picking up the shell . . . that's when I was poisoned. Could the kraken have been a delusion? But even Henwyneb heard its cry. Unless it really was a horse being butchered on the beach. Nia said she came to find me because of the shell. Was the shell a trap set for me? But why would she want to work a trick like that on me? I don't have anything worth stealing. No, I've become as full of fear as the king.*

Corwin put his fists to his forehead, feeling the scar of the sun-shaped mark on his palm pinching his skin. He glanced down at his hand. *She has this same mark, and she's also poisoned. I felt the thoughts of the Farworlder prince before I even met Nia.* There was a tiny sliver in his palm from the block of wood holding the candle that he had summoned to his hand the night before. *Aha. That is no illusion.*

Concentrating with all his mind, Corwin tried to find Nia's thoughts. She was frightened and angry. Her skin felt dry and hot, and she wished desperately to immerse herself in water. She was worried about him. *Nia,* he thought, *some men are trying to tell me you're a liar. Show me Atlantis.*

He received no words in return, but an image flooded his mind of a beautiful city glimmering with pale green lights in the dark depths of the sea. Tall palaces covered with shells and coral. Dolphins and enormous sea turtles swimming side by side with mermyds. He shared her memories of swimming through tall, carved pillars of stone, of being swept along a current of fast water in a cloud of bubbles. He could taste the seaweed and fish she ate, the kelpwine she drank. *This is a place far more wonderful than I could've ever imagined. If this is an illusion, then so's my entire life.*

Calmly Corwin raised his head. "I'm sorry, good sirs, but I believe Nia," he stated firmly. "I *have* shared her thoughts. I know she isn't lying. And I can't possibly do what you ask for the king." *And I can't believe I'm being this high-principled. Fenwyck must be spinning in his cage.*

"You realize what you're saying, boy?" Anguis asked with a solemn frown. "The dire consequences of your words? Your life hangs in the balance, as does that of your lady friend."

"We're doomed already. If the creature in the shell is killed, then she and I will die, too. If she dies, the creature and I die. Our fates are joined. There's no point in saving only one or two of us."

The mages stared at him as if he had sprouted a second head.

At that moment, King Vortigern strode in, accompanied only by two guardsmen. "Well, my lords, has your pet prognosticator seen the light of reason?"

"Alas, no," Anguis said, still staring at Corwin with a glint of pity in his eyes. "It would appear this young man has lost the use of his reason. He believes he will die when the creature in the shell dies, or the girl. I fear he will be of no use to us, Your Majesty."

"Didn't I predict that he would be useless?" Vortigern asked smugly. "I have become a better seer than you, Anguis. Very well. If he thinks he will die when the girl does, let them die together. Put him in the cage with her."

Corwin felt surprisingly calm. Perhaps the feeling was left over from the peace of the underwater world he had experienced through Nia's thoughts. Perhaps it was that his strength was spent. He no longer had the energy to be frightened or angry. He did consider leaping on the king and delivering some stiff blows to that smug face. Then they'd have a really *good* reason to execute him. But instead Corwin let the guards lead him away like a chastised puppy.

They guided him roughly out through the courtyard. All the courtiers loitering there pointed and stared at him as he passed. He noticed Lord Faustus, especially, laughing at him with a vulpine grin. Corwin felt as though he were six years old again and being exhibited as "the Wild Boy of Caledonia."

He was led out to the castle wall. To his shock, they had put Nia in the same cage that Fenwyck . . . still inhabited. The cage was lowered, and the locked gate was opened. Nia sat curled up at the far rim, as far from the musty-smelling pile of bones and flies and tattered cloth as she could make herself. Her pale skin was beginning to redden in patches, and her hair looked brittle as straw.

Corwin was unceremoniously pushed in. He had to scramble to neither crush Fenwyck's bones, nor Nia. As he squeezed himself in tight between the living and the dead, Corwin stared at the remnants of what had once been the only father he had ever known. He was so drained he could only feel a distant sorrow as he stared at the stained and frayed "Hammurabian" robe, and the wrinkled, sun-browned skin that still clung to the skull and arms. Only a few wispy gray strands of hair remained on the top of Fenwyck's head. The eyes were gone, no doubt plucked by some of Nag's cousins. "You never looked better, old man," Corwin said, but the jest felt hollow.

The cage door was slammed shut with a loud clang. The winch was turned, tightening the thick rope, and the cage was hauled up and up, high on the castle wall.

There was no shelter from the burning late-summer sun, and it beat down upon Corwin and Nia with unrelieved intensity. The stone castle wall beside them reflected more heat into the cage, making it feel as hot as an oven. The cage wasn't tall enough for Corwin to stand and shade Nia. He tried to crouch over her, but the shifting of his weight made the cage tilt, sending Fenwyck's bones sliding into Nia's leg. She made a little shriek and pulled herself tighter against the bars of the cage. Laughter drifted up from the guards and onlookers below. Corwin took off his shirt and tied the sleeves to the bars, but this only provided a small patch of shade, constantly disrupted by the wind.

"Now your skin will be burned," Nia said, sadly.

"It doesn't really matter," Corwin said. "Once the prince goes into the stewpot, we'll know what it's like to be boiled alive instead of baked. Nia, I'm so sorry. This is all my fault. I never should have taken that shell from within the leviathan. Or I should have dropped it once I saw the kraken. You might have retrieved it then."

But Nia weakly shook her head. "Ma'el would have gotten it then, and we would already be dead. You gave us a chance. And we needed you to complete the Naming."

"I'm afraid I wasted our last chance," Corwin said, the shame rising in him. "The king's wizards might have spared us if I'd been willing to use my visions to find rebels Vortigern could execute. But I couldn't do it." Corwin looked down at the remains of Fenwyck, almost expecting the skull to laugh at him.

Nia gave him a small smile. "You are brave and kind. I told you our prince chose wisely."

Corwin blushed and looked away. "To choose an idiot like me? If I had even pretended to believe that you had lied to me about Atlantis, the mages might not have let me go so easily. They still think that your city never existed, except as a myth or an island destroyed by cataclysm."

Nia let out a bitter laugh. "How strange that Atlantis has written its own fate. We are taught in our history that land-dwellers threatened our peace and so we sank beneath the waves to avoid them. We let stories be spread around the world that Atlantis was destroyed by angry gods, so that no one would come searching for us. And now, when Atlantis needs the help of land-dwellers, no one believes we exist."

"Why is it that when we try hardest to help ourselves, we somehow end up dooming ourselves instead?" Corwin muttered. He looked again at what was left of Fenwyck. This time the skull appeared to be grinning mockingly back.

Chapter Eight

The minutes crawled slowly by as the sun reached its zenith in the sky. Corwin's threadbare shirt wasn't doing much to hold the merciless rays at bay. Nia's skin was visibly drying—patches of bare skin on her arms were beginning to look as lifeless as Fenwyck's. Corwin's mouth felt parched. The River Twy gurgled not far away, flowing beside the castle to form part of its moat. Its liquid laughter was tantalizing, and Corwin dearly wished he could taste its brackish water on his tongue. *It must be torment for Nia*, he thought, *who probably wishes she could be swimming in it.*

"Why aren't we dead yet?" Corwin asked no one in particular. "They must have put the shell in the soup pot by now."

"I don't know," Nia whispered. "The prince . . . has found bits of seaweed on which he can feed. He has a little strength now, and he is using his powers to make people nearby forget he is there. It's all he can do."

"I'm not sure that's better, if it just prolongs our agony. Can his powers help us escape from this cage?"

"I . . . don't know the mechanism of this lock. If you do, perhaps we . . . ," she drifted off weakly while staring at the cage door.

"No," Corwin said. "You're too sapped of strength already. An open door won't help if we're unconscious. Besides, the fall to the ground might kill us, and if it didn't, the guards below would just hoist us up again."

Corwin leaned back against the hot iron bars and closed his eyes. *If only I could have a vision of what to do here.*

Touch the prince's mind, Nia said or thought to him; Corwin wasn't sure which. *Let him aid you.*

Corwin calmed his mind and tried to allow in the thoughts of the alien Farworlder-mind. As before, he sensed the prince was floating in tepid water, free of the shell and swimming around a little. It was actually pleasant, this time, to visit the prince's thoughts for a while. The little leviathan was in a more comfortable place, at least at the moment. *Can you tell me where you are?*

To Corwin's amazement, he could now see out of the Farworlder's eyes. He saw the surface of the water breaking above him, saw slender little pink tentacles reach up the side of the . . . bucket, Corwin guessed, felt himself/the prince crawling out to perch on the rim. The prince's eyes looked around. Almost everything was unfamiliar to the Farworlder, but Corwin could tell him what he was seeing. *Yes, this bucket seems to be sitting on a table. That smoky cave with a fire in it is a hearth where meals are cooked. That's a sideboard on which meals are prepared, vegetables cut, that sort of thing. That looks like a lump of bread dough. No, it's not alive. That's a woman, she's dressed like a servant . . . probably a cook. She's yawning, wiping her hands on her apron, and leaving. That's good, maybe she won't come back. And at least she won't see us . . . you.*

The eyes of the prince gazed down. The kitchen floor looked a long way off to the tiny Farworlder, even if he were to leap to the tabletop first. *Probably not a good idea for you to make a break for it,* Corwin advised. *Not if you can't stay out of water long. Castles are big and easy to get lost in, even for a land-dweller.*

With an inward, squidlike equivalent of a sigh, the Farworlder prince let go of the side of the bucket and slid back into the water. He found his shell and slipped back inside.

I was hoping to ask you, Corwin thought on, *whether you had any idea of what we can do, any sense of the unis.*

No, the prince's thoughts came back. *Only smoke, fire, and water. That's all I see.*

Then I guess we're all doomed. With that sad thought, Corwin returned his attention to his own body, still in the cage. The heat was oppressive and he ached all over. He'd rather have stayed in the bucket with the prince.

"Ma'el," Nia murmured, "must have killed . . . the High Council . . . for their oculae . . . the seat of their magic power. He wants them all. Any . . . still out of his control . . . can interfere. I have a partial oculus. The prince still has one. We can stop Ma'el . . . perhaps. That's why he wants to destroy us."

Poor thing, Corwin thought. *The heat must be addling her mind. What good is it to worry about her evil king now, when my evil king is certain to destroy us sooner? And even if he doesn't, and the prince somehow escapes notice, the toxins in our blood will kill us in five days. I hope Atlantis has a better chance of rescue than we do.*

"Raaawk!"

Corwin opened one eye. "You again. Come to gloat, have you?"

"Raaawk!" replied Nag.

"What do you mean, it's my own fault?" Corwin asked

drowsily. He was almost beginning to think he understood the bird.

"Graaa-awwk!"

"Intended to be useful? If you want to be useful, go
fetch us the key to the cage."

"Braa-werk!"

"Well, a guard has it, stupid. Or if you can't fetch that,
at least bring us a waterskin. Or a scrap of food."

"Nawk! Nawk!"

"What do you mean, I'm the stupid one? What am *I*
supposed to do?"

With an exasperated shake of his head, Nag hopped
into the cage and began to tug at Fenwyck's tattered
sleeve.

"Here, now, stop that! Don't eat the man who fed you!
Besides, others before you have already taken the good
parts. Shoo!" Corwin flicked his hand and sent the raven
flying away, cawing indignantly.

"Useless bird," Corwin grumbled. He closed his eyes
again and dozed. The heat of the summer day leeched the
last of his strength and he fell into dreams—dreams of
being a loaf of bread baking or a fresh-forged sword blade
being hammered by a blacksmith.

The blacksmith turned into Fenwyck, as he had been

in life. "Foolish boy. Have you forgotten everything I taught you?" Fenwyck cuffed him as he so often had.

"Ow! What have I forgotten?" Corwin whined in his dream.

"Everything! You forgot to say nice things! You forgot how people see what they want to see and believe what they want to believe. Don't you remember our tricks from the old days?" A memory returned to Corwin of how he would stick his head in a barrel of water, holding his breath.

"Oh, I really wish I could do that right now," Corwin said.

"But you can. Remember this one?" There was the memory of Fenwyck raising his hands dramatically and fire appearing on a piece of parchment on the stage. Unseen by the audience was the little burning glass that Fenwyck always kept hidden in his sleeve.

"Didn't I once tell you," Fenwyck went on, "that only those who believe they are defeated *are* defeated?" The flames grew to encompass the entire stage, surrounding Fenwyck. He began to burn, his skin darkening and shrinking.

Corwin did remember. "Yes, as we were running away from a pack of bakers who were angry because you had stolen a meat pie from their booth."

"And we had a fine meal that afternoon, didn't we?" Fenwyck said, as the flames melted him into the dried-out husk that Corwin now shared the iron cage with.

Corwin coughed and sat up suddenly, awake once more. He wondered how long he had slept. The sun was somewhat lower in the sky. Nia lay sprawled completely unconscious, her skin red as a beet. Corwin looked at Fenwyck's remains and saw the fresh tear Nag had made in his dead mentor's sleeve—the sleeve where the old conniver had usually carried the burning glass.

Corwin reached over and felt along the hem of the sleeve. Sure enough, he found a bulge in a tiny pocket in the hem. Corwin pulled out the little lens. "All right, old man, I've found it. Now what shall I burn?"

He looked around, and then up. Corwin saw the rope from which the cage hung. It was a little frayed where it was knotted around the iron loop at the top of the cage. *Yes, that'll burn,* Corwin thought, *but if it breaks and we drop, it'll just mean we die a little sooner.*

Glancing over the side of the cage, Corwin saw that the ground below slanted toward the River Twy. *If we could manage to roll into the water, then we might float far enough, fast enough, to evade the guards.*

Guards? Corwin looked farther and noticed that the

gate guards were gone. The townsfolk who had watched and jeered were also gone, no doubt escaping the hot summer sun. *If I'm going to do anything, it had better be now.*

Corwin pulled himself up into a crouch, careful not to set the cage to swinging. He stood as high as he dared without tilting the cage. Gripping the little burning glass tightly, he raised his hand through the top bars of the cage. He turned his hand this way and that to best catch the rays of the afternoon sun, finally holding the lens just so as a tiny but intense bright dot appeared on the rope.

Corwin's leg muscles shuddered with the effort of holding himself in such an awkward stance. He gritted his teeth, worried that his limbs would give way at any moment.

At last, a tendril of smoke wafted out of the rope. Corwin nearly cried out in triumph as tiny flames flickered among the frayed ends. Pressing his face against the top of the cage, Corwin blew gently on the rope as he would to encourage a campfire.

To his joy, the tiny flames rapidly grew and grew until they engulfed the length of rope above the cage. Corwin crouched down again and gently shook Nia's shoulder.

"Nia, Nia, wake up! We might be able to get free."

She stirred a little, but her eyes didn't open.

"Nia, we'll be falling soon. We have to be ready."

When she didn't respond, Corwin gathered her into his arms, laying her head on his shoulder. He looked up at the rope and waited.

Long minutes passed, and then the cage suddenly broke free. Corwin curled up around Nia, holding her tightly, yelling as the cage fell. It turned sideways as it fell, and hit the ground with a metallic *gungggggg*. Pain shot up Corwin's left side as he hit the cage bars half a moment later. The cage rolled, rumbling down the embankment, knocking his arms, legs, and head around as he tumbled within, still holding Nia. Fenwyck's skull and bones clattered against the bars with a merry rattle.

The cold water of the river shocked his skin as the cage splashed into the Twy. It came to rest on its side on the riverbank, the water flowing through the bars. Corwin shuddered, letting go of Nia. She suddenly awoke with a surprised gasp and splashed and rolled in the water. Corwin was amazed to see how quickly her skin began to heal and her strength to return.

The door to the cage, as luck would have it, was now overhead. "Nia, if you're well enough, let's try to open the lock."

She nodded and they both stood, pressing their hands

against the cage door. But the cage was on uneven ground and with a shriek they fell forward. The cage rolled again, tumbling them farther into the river, where it promptly sank into deep water.

Corwin gasped one last deep breath before his head was pushed below the surface by the bars of the cage. The cage sank swiftly, and he felt it strike bottom within moments. But it didn't stop there. The powerful current of the River Twy pushed against the cage and Corwin and Nia, bouncing and rolling them along the riverbed.

The cage came to a sudden stop, lodged against a huge boulder. But Corwin saw that the topmost bars were still beneath the surface. Air bubbles trapped in Fenwyck's robe made the old man's remains float and waggle at the top of the cage with a bizarre semblance of life.

Corwin pushed the corpse aside and lunged up against the iron bars, hoping he could at least bob up to get air, but the cage was too heavy and wedged tight against the boulder. Below him, Corwin could see Nia desperately fumbling at the lock of the cage door.

Corwin was good at holding his breath. He had studied the insides of many a barrel with his head underwater as Fenwyck blathered to the crowd about "The Boy Who Breathes Water." But he could feel his lungs screaming for air as the last bubbles streamed out of his nose. Gently pulling Nia aside from the cage door he kicked at it with the last of his strength. But the lock held firm.

Corwin moaned, knowing at any moment he was going to gasp for air and drink water instead and drown. He felt something move over his face—Nia's lips pressed hard against his.

A kiss good-bye, he thought. *Well, there are worse ends.* He allowed his lips to part, to meet hers—

And suddenly a blast of air entered his mouth, filling his cheeks. Corwin gasped with surprise, nearly swallowing water as Nia pressed harder against him. He saw the gills on her neck flapping furiously in the water.

Stay calm, he heard in his mind. *Breathe, and let me give you air.*

Of course! Corwin realized as he let himself relax in the water and enjoy the experience of receiving air from a beautiful girl's mouth. *She's a mermaid, and for her the water is life-giving, not life-taking.*

Chapter Nine

The cold of the River Twy didn't matter, with the rush of
Nia's breath in Corwin's mouth and the warmth of her
lips on his. It took him some moments to realize that they
now had all the time they needed to open the cage door.
Nia pulled away first and pointed at the lock. "Let's keep
trying," she said, quite clearly, though they were underwater.

Corwin felt newly at ease, as though he were a merman himself, as he swam up to the lock of the iron cage
and inspected it. Fenwyck had taught him about all sorts
of locks. This one was simple—two tumblers were all that
needed to move. With the right tool, it would be quick
work. This time, however, he would have to move them
with his mind.

Corwin felt himself running out of air again and
turned to Nia. He went eagerly to her lips, giving her a
kiss that was, well, more a kiss than taking a breath of air.
Nia playfully blew a blast into his mouth and pinched his

cheek. Her eyes held an expression of both amusement and warning as he pulled away again.

"We have to concentrate on saving the prince," she said. "Remember, our lives still depend upon it."

Corwin nodded regretfully and went back to examining the lock. Nia placed her hand over his. Corwin felt an amazing surge of power come from her hand, coursing through his skin and the tendons of his fingers. He felt Nia bring in the Farworlder prince as a presence in their thoughts. The three of them together concentrated on the lock. Although it wasn't expressed in words, the leviathan imparted to Corwin how to use the power now surging through his hand to "sense" where the lock mechanisms were. Corwin closed his eyes and discovered that the energy field from his hand could, in a way, see and touch the tumblers in the lock. Since water was easier to move than iron, Corwin found that he could push on the water within the lock to shift the tumblers aside.

Soon there came a loud, satisfying *click* from the lock, and the cage door drifted open. Nia gestured toward the opening, indicating that Corwin should leave first. He swam out of the cage with mixed feelings, glad to be free, but sad that he wouldn't have the chance to kiss Nia again. *Not for a while, but maybe when this is all over . . .*

His head broke the surface of the river, and he gulped down air. He had to grab quickly for the top of the boulder as the current of the Twy tried to pull him downriver.

Apparently his motion in the water had pulled what was left of Fenwyck out of the cage, and the sodden remains bobbed to the surface. The body, quite beyond grasping any boulders itself, was caught by the current and went merrily spinning away, as if Fenwyck, too, were happy to be free. "Farewell, old man," Corwin murmured. "May your various pieces find peace somewhere."

Just as Corwin was getting concerned that he had not seen Nia emerge from the cage, he heard something like the spouting of a small whale behind him. "There you are!" he said as she grabbed onto the boulder beside him.

"I was enjoying the swim," Nia said with a smile.

Corwin was amazed at how beautiful she looked now that the water had again worked its restorative wonders upon her. "Um, I'm . . . glad. I'm enjoying the view."

She splashed him playfully. "It's time to think of our next step." She turned and swam to the far bank and Corwin followed, finding it difficult to turn his thoughts at all.

But as he crawled up onto the riverbank, a wave of nausea came over him and the world spun, reminding him of the poison still in his body. *It's not enough that we just made it through something incredibly difficult. We're still facing the impossible in order to survive at all.* He dared a glance back over his shoulder at the castle. The area beneath where the cage had hung was still deserted.

Someone must have heard us fall and strike the ground. Why hasn't anyone come out to investigate? Fenwyck had often told him never to look a gift horse in the mouth. But Corwin also knew the saying "Never buy a sack of gold dust without sifting it for sand."

He realized he could ask the Farworlder prince if he knew what was going on in the castle. *What's happening?* he asked the prince.

I am tired. I cannot do the forgetfulness spell much longer. Come find me.

Corwin staggered farther up the bank to where Nia had crawled into a den of bushes. She looked like a forest nymph with leaves and sticks in her long, pale hair. "The prince doesn't know how much longer he can keep the forgetfulness spell working," she said.

"Yes, I heard," Corwin said. "I get the feeling that something strange is going on at the castle, but of course our little prince can't see much of the world from his bucket."

"We have to get to him soon."

"That's easier said than done," Corwin muttered, staring at the high stone castle walls and thick, iron-banded gate. "If we try to go in through the front way, we'll just be recaptured."

Nia pulled up a river reed from the bank and chewed on it thoughtfully. She stared at the castle with such determination that Corwin felt she would melt the walls down with her gaze if she could.

"Maybe there's another entrance," she said at last. "In my city, I had a . . . friend, a former friend, who taught me that there are doors and entries that workers know of that nobles don't. And there can be portals for other purposes that can be used as doors."

Corwin felt another wash of emotion from her, memories of someone, a dark-haired young merman. Her thoughts were filled with love and fear and hate. Corwin received vague images of this merman swimming through a maze of tunnels . . . and he suddenly remembered what the mages had said about the labyrinths of catacombs and waterways beneath the castle. Prince Vortimer and Faustus had talked about them while in Henwyneb's cottage. "Nia, you could be right," he said. "The king's son mentioned there were viaducts leading off from the river into the castle. If we can find those, we may be able to swim into the cisterns beneath. And from there maybe we can find an entrance into the castle itself."

"That's a great idea!" Nia burst out. "I'll be stronger if we can stay in water. And no one will expect us to come that way. If we enter when it's dark, we might get in without being seen."

Corwin was flattered by her praise. But he noticed that the afternoon was fast fading into evening. Already the stones of the castle were tinged gold with the westering sunlight. "Wait until dark? But if we stay in water, won't the kraken follow us, once the sun has set?"

Alarm passed across Nia's face like a shadow. "I'd forgotten about Ma'el's creature. Since we're still alive, it'll be searching for us. Once darkness falls, he could send it up the river."

Corwin felt his stomach turn at the thought of seeing the huge scarlet snake again. It would be harder to run away from the narrow confines of the river. And this time he didn't have a heavy bag of shells to bash the monster in the head with. "I'd really rather not be the welcoming party for it when he does. Maybe we should take the chance of being seen and go now, before sunset."

"I agree," Nia said. "Sooner is better, if we can succeed."

Corwin glanced all around. There were still no guards or village sightseers nearby. He was beginning to find such luck unnerving. "Okay, then. This seems like a good time."

Nia stood and ran gracefully to the river, then slipped into the water as smoothly as a seal. Corwin followed, but not so gracefully. He *really* hoped no one was watching as he blundered, splashed, and stumbled his way through the muck of the riverbank and fell back into the shallows. The water felt more chill this time, and Corwin's teeth began to chatter. Nia's head went underwater and she kicked like the flash of a dolphin's fluke, and then she was gone.

Corwin tried to swim, but they were heading upriver, and the current was too strong. He had to be satisfied with pulling himself along by the rocks, or crawling in the shallow water of the river when he couldn't. He kept a wary eye on the narrow slit windows of the castle, and the crenellated parapets, but he didn't see any watchful faces along the wall.

Corwin started to worry when he hadn't seen Nia for a few minutes. The river sucked at his ankles; the mud pulled at his feet; the bushes on the riverbank tore at his hair, his clothing, and his skin. His hands and knees were nearly numb from the cold water. He wondered if this plan had been the right choice, but realized it would have been far worse if they'd waited for dark.

He wanted to call out Nia's name but didn't dare. Although he couldn't see anyone, that didn't mean there wasn't anyone in hearing distance who could come running. *Why had she just swum off? Why hasn't she waited for me? Where has she gone? Well, she can't have died, because I'm still alive, but that doesn't mean she isn't in trouble. Wouldn't my mind know it if she were in trouble? If she'd been knocked unconscious, would I know it? This is all too strange.*

Just as Corwin was about to risk discovery and shout for her, Nia rose out of the water before him. "Where have you been?" he yelled before he could stop himself.

She blinked, startled. "I searched for the place where the river enters the castle," she said. "I found it, but I wanted to warn you: It could be dangerous for you."

"Oh." *I'm an idiot. She was doing something useful, and I just shouted at her.* "Um, I'm sorry. I mean, that's good. Finding the entrance, I mean. Not the danger part. Um, what's the danger part?"

"The river enters the castle through a small . . . tunnel, I think you'd call it," Nia said, ignoring his awkwardness.

"It's completely full of water. You won't be able to breathe on your own. And the water runs so swiftly through it that we may not be able to swim out if we become trapped. At the end there seems to be a . . . a gate with bars, like our cage. I don't know how or if it can be opened."

"Show me where it is and we'll see what we can do."

Her brow furrowed in thought. It was the prettiest frown Corwin had ever seen. "It will be best for you," she said, "to go up the stream farther and then cross. That way the current will carry you to the place where we should enter, but not past it."

Corwin roughly grasped what she meant. "Okay. But you have to show me where the entrance is so that I can aim for it."

"Keep your gaze on me, then," she said, diving back into the river.

"How could I not?" Corwin murmured, watching her silvery hair and dress flash through the water, as though she were a giant fish. In mere moments she appeared at the other bank, the castle wall rising above her. She waved, and Corwin hoped no one saw her.

He staggered farther upriver, choosing a place from which he was certain he could reach Nia in a swift swim.

He dove into the deeper water and began to swim as hard as he could. But the strength of the current amazed him, carrying him faster than he had imagined. Corwin was too afraid to stop swimming and look around. But it seemed to take forever, stroke after stroke in the murky, cold water, and still he hadn't reached the other bank, and again he was running out of air.

A hand grasped his arm. And pulled. It was Nia, who had anchored her leg to a huge iron ring underwater. She tugged him close to her, pointed at a circle of brick and mortar, and placed his hand at the edge of the tunnel. The current wasn't so strong here, but still Corwin had to make sure his grip on the side of the circle was secure before he surfaced.

Their heads came out of the water at the same time. There was a loud gurgle from the very top of the tunnel, which curved just above the waterline. "Oh, I'm so glad. I nearly lost you," Nia said.

"Lucky for me you didn't," Corwin said. "I don't think the river would've let me go until it reached Carmarthen Bay."

"Yes," Nia agreed. "This river reminds me of the bubble-flow tunnels of Atlantis. They also have swift and dangerous currents." Once more, Corwin sensed the overwhelming sadness Nia felt about what had happened to her before they met, and he glimpsed the vision of the dark-haired merman again. This time, he got a sharp understanding that it wasn't just sorrow, fear, and anger that the memory brought up in her—there was some kind of guilt and shame mixed in as well. He wondered if he would ever know the details of Nia's mystery.

"An underwater city has rivers?" Corwin asked, trying to distract her from her pain.

"Yes," Nia answered. "Water can move within water. Even the great oceans have currents that are mighty undersea rivers. One of them passes near the shore of your land."

"I see," he said with a nod. "So is this the only river culvert you've found?"

"Yes," Nia said.

"Then we'd better try it."

"If we hold on to each other," Nia offered, "then I can still help you breathe even if we're trapped."

Corwin didn't mind that idea at all. He gladly let Nia wrap her arms around his chest. "You'll stay close if I need to breathe?" he asked.

Nia scowled at him, but also smiled. "For the prince," she reminded him gently.

Corwin sighed. "Yes, right. For the prince." He took several deep breaths to take as much air into his lungs as he could. Then he dove into the brick circle, holding Nia tightly to him.

The speed of the water in the tube was amazing. The tunnel angled down, the water flowing ever faster as it went. Corwin felt his back scrape against the brick and wished he'd retrieved his shirt before escaping the cage. His head banged against a curve of the tunnel, and he would have cried out if he'd dared open his mouth. In only moments his shoulder struck something hard, and he grabbed an iron bar.

Suddenly he was swinging out over open air, the grate having pulled out of one side. Nia slid down him, shoved along by the waterfall pouring out of the tube, until she was hanging by his ankle. She shrieked, and the sound echoed through a large, empty cavern.

Corwin willed his eyes to adjust to the darkness as he held on for dear life. They were in a giant cistern whose vaulted ceiling, held up by slender pillars, was higher than the largest hall in the castle. On distant walls, torches provided the only illumination.

Corwin's hand slipped, and he didn't know how much longer he could hold on, carrying both their weight. "Nia, can you see how deep the water is below you?" If it were deep enough, he could safely let go. If it were shallow, the floor beneath might break their bones.

"I'll find out," she said, letting her hand slip.

"No! Wait! Nia!"

There came a splash and then a silence filled only with the roar of the falling water behind him. "Nia!"

A pale nimbus of hair broke the water below. "It's three man-heights deep," Nia called up to him. "You can fall."

Corwin groaned, grateful that Nia was okay, and then opened his hand. It took two seconds before his feet struck the water below and he plunged deep into the cold water of the cistern. As soon as he could, he kicked and swam to the surface. "I wish you wouldn't do that," he said as he emerged beside Nia.

"Do what? Oh, look, we're not alone." Nia reached down, then held up a flapping fish in one hand.

"Go off and try dangerous things. Um. Never mind." *I keep forgetting how she's from another world.*

"This is an ocean fish," Nia said, "so there must be another entrance into this place that's closer to the sea." She let the fish go. "The prince is this way," she said, nodding in one direction.

"How do you know?" Corwin asked. "I'm as tied to the prince as you are, and I have no idea how to get to the kitchens from here."

Nia tilted her head again. "Don't you feel the earth pulling on your body? Don't you feel the . . ." She struggled for words a moment. "It's like water current, only very faint and gentle. It always flows to what you call north."

"I have no idea what you're talking about."

"Let the prince show you."

Corwin grabbed hold of a broken piece of pillar sticking out of the water and let his mind join the Farworlder again. *What is this current Nia's talking about?*

Suddenly his body tingled, and he felt an ever-so-subtle tugging within him. For a moment, faint lines of light flickered before his eyes, through everything around him, even Nia.

"Almost all large creatures of the sea feel this," Nia said. "It's how they find their feeding and mating grounds."

Corwin suddenly understood, and he, too, knew that the prince was up that way and over to the right. But he never would have been able to explain to anyone in words how he knew this. "Is this another one of those magical powers we get from being joined to the prince?"

Nia laughed. "It's not magic. It's one of the most ordinary things in the world, in the sea."

I'm sure the sea would seem like a very magical place to me, Corwin thought. This new sense of orientation was a great relief, since he didn't relish the idea of becoming lost in the gloomy, watery, underworld hall. Fenwyck had once told him of the old Roman story about the River Styx, which one had to cross in order to reach the afterlife. *From the looks of this cistern, it could surely be the antechamber to Hades.* "Let's move on. But please stay close this time, so I know where you are."

"I'll be just ahead," Nia said, "and I'll make it easy for you to see me." She shot off like an arrow to their left, a strange, greenish phosphorescence glowing in her wake and along her body. Corwin swam after her, amazed at how she continued to surprise him. The Farworlder-prince-voice said, *This glow is the same power that can raise the kraken, but not as strong.*

You no longer sound like a child, princeling, Corwin thought.

Being joined to the two of you, I am learning very fast.

So am I. As his eyes adjusted to the dim light, Corwin could see that not all the columns were in perfect repair. Indeed, some of them were cracked and a few were broken, leaving piles of stone to scrape the unwary shin. Vortimer was right, Corwin had to admit. With the

Romans long gone, and no one knowing how to repair such structures, it was no wonder that a tower built above it would fall. Corwin wished he could be more certain that the ceiling overhead itself would hold.

As he swam by a broken pillar, accidentally kicking it with his foot, a chunk of stone and masonry fell off and splashed in the water behind him.

"Skreee! Skreee! Skreee!" The high-pitched shrieking echoed through the cistern as a black, living cloud descended from the high, vaulted ceiling.

"The kraken!" Corwin cried, and he ducked underwater, then realized the idiocy of that move and surfaced again. He looked wildly around for escape.

Nia was staring up, fascinated. Corwin dared to look up, too. And felt extremely foolish. It was merely a host of bats that had been disturbed by the sound of the falling rock. The bats fluttered this way and that, zooming between the pillars, until they finally departed or resettled on the ceiling.

"I knew it wasn't the kraken," Nia said, "because those aren't creatures of the sea. But I can't tell what they are. Are they like your bird, Nag?"

"No," Corwin grumbled, annoyed with himself. "They're bats. Mice with wings, really. Mostly harmless."

Nia began to laugh. "And you thought—"

"Yes, yes, I thought it might be the kraken. I'm sorry if I'm a little jumpy. Now can we move along while I'm still wearing my skin?"

Still giggling and grinning, Nia turned and continued to swim. Corwin followed, feeling his face grow red with embarrassment. *How many more times can I make a fool of myself before she decides her prince didn't choose wisely? I shouldn't have been caught up in all this, anyway. I don't have any special talents, other than useless visions and picking pockets at county fairs. I'll bet once we get to the prince and heal ourselves, she'll take her little squidling and return to the sea and I'll just be a joke she'll tell to the other mermaids. There was this landdweller named Corwin. . . .*

Something slimy, like a tendril of seaweed or an eel, brushed against his right ankle and began to close around his foot. Corwin shook his leg, and it let go. It grabbed his other leg, wrapping more tightly. Corwin angrily kicked at it hard with his free foot and it let go. He swam as fast as he could after Nia. *It was nothing*, he told himself. *I'm not going to tell her about it. She already thinks I'm cowardly and stupid. She'd just laugh and tell me it was a strand of waterweeds. Which it probably was.* Although that wasn't what it had felt like. Corwin didn't want to think about what it had felt like.

It seemed they swam for a long time through the vast, echoing cistern. Corwin lost his sense of time, and that wasn't something the Farworlder prince could help him with, as he was occupied with guiding Nia and Corwin to him. Nia continued to swim just ahead, glowing eerily green.

But at last they came to a wall in which there was an archway. Beneath the arch were stone stairs leading up from the water. Fortunately, the iron portcullis gate in the arch that might have blocked their way had been raised. Nia nimbly pulled herself out of the water and sat on the step just above the waterline.

As Corwin crawled up onto the stairs, he felt another wave of weakness and nausea strike him. He had to lie on the cold stone for long moments as the world spun around him.

Nia touched his shoulder. "It's the poison. We can only hold off its effects for so long."

"Then . . . what are we . . . waiting for?" growled Corwin. "Let's hurry."

Nia put an arm around his shoulders and helped him stand. "We will heal each other. Come on."

They staggered up the slippery steps, curving around one flight, then two. There was a wooden door at the top, but this wasn't locked. They entered a short hallway whose air was full of the aroma of baking bread and cooking vegetables. "Well," Corwin gasped. "It seems like we just need to follow our noses to find the kitchens."

They crept along the hall until they found the doorway leading into a large room. Corwin recognized it as if he had been there before. Which in a sense he had. A fire burned merrily in the enormous hearth, where a huge black kettle hung over the flames. In the center of the room was the trestle table, on which sat the wooden bucket. No one else was in the room, fortunately. A pile of partially cut onions lay, along with a butcher knife, on the side table. The lump of bread dough sat nearby, gathering flies.

"Our prince's forgetting spell must have worked very well," Corwin said. "Royal kitchens are usually crowded with cooks and servants."

"Look, there he is!" Nia cried.

A little bulbous head with big eyes poked up over the rim of the bucket and a little tentacle waved tentatively at them.

Both Corwin and Nia rushed to the table.

"He's grown so much!" Nia exclaimed. She scooped him up out of the bucket.

"So that's what he looks like," Corwin murmured. The prince did indeed look like a tiny leviathan. His skin was a pinkish-green, and he was a bit longer than Nia's hand. His yellow-green eyes blinked at them.

Glad to see you. Glad to see you.

Corwin couldn't help smiling. "Glad to see you, too."

"But for his protection, we'd better put him back in his shell," Nia said.

Corwin fished the shiny, silvery shell out of the bucket. Nia held the prince over the shell and let the creature slither back in. Corwin was amazed the little leviathan fit.

"Now we must do the Naming," Nia went on.

"Wait a moment," Corwin said. He went to each doorway in the kitchen and closed the doors. "We don't want anyone passing by to see us," he explained. He couldn't find a way to lock the doors, though, so he hoped they could get the spell done quickly.

"So now what do we do?" he asked when he returned to the table.

"It's never been done with three before," Nia replied, "at least, not that I know of. So I'll have to guess. First, sit."

They sat on either side of the table, Nia cradling the shell in her hands, Corwin placing his hands over hers.

"Now we must combine our energies," Nia said, "first to heal the prince, then to heal ourselves. Do you remember the flame-in-hand that you saw me do back at the inn?"

Corwin nodded, still impressed with that particular magic.

"That's how it's done. Send all the energy of your body into your hands. Send it from your hands into the shell, give it to the prince, and he will heal himself."

Corwin bowed his head and closed his eyes. He wasn't sure how to gather energy at all. It wasn't like gathering seashells, he was certain. *Let me help*, came the princeling's thoughts in his mind. Suddenly Corwin *did* know how. He concentrated first on his feet and legs and felt a surge of warmth flow upward through them. The warmth entered his belly and chest, gathering there, stronger and stronger. Warmth flowed down from his shoulders and arms as well to join it. Finally Corwin could hold it in no longer, and the energy flowed out into his hands as though it were water, pouring into Nia's hands and into the shell.

Nia's hands had grown hot as well, and Corwin could

feel the air heat up around them. Corwin feared at first his hands would be burned, but this human fire was not destructive. It felt marvelous, like he could bask in it forever.

"Remember, we must heal the prince," Nia murmured, "before we heal ourselves."

Again, Corwin was at a momentary loss about what to do next. But it didn't matter. He could feel the Farworlder taking the energy into himself, transforming himself. Corwin risked opening his eyes for just a peek. The shell was glowing, iridescent. A cloud of sparkling light swirled around it. As Corwin watched, the little squid-prince floated out of the shell as if swimming in the flow of energy. The creature itself glowed from within, and it floated above the shell, drifting in circles, soaking in the healing energy. It was a beautiful sight.

Corwin could feel, secondhand, the effort that the Farworlder was using to heal himself. How the energy burned like sweet fire in his tentacles and head. Finally, with an *ahhhhhhh*, the prince's work was done—he had purified his blood of the poisonous fluid. He flowed back into the shell, taking much of the energy cloud with him.

"Is it done?" Corwin whispered.

"Shhh," Nia said. "Next it's our turn."

The shell glowed brighter and brighter until it hurt Corwin's eyes to look at it. Suddenly the light exploded, pouring out over Corwin and Nia, swirling around them as it had the shell. Corwin gasped deeply as the energy entered him, warmed his skin, sang in his blood. He now felt the sweet fire directly, burning in his bones. He wanted to smile and scream, to howl with joy and pain. He felt himself changing, although he didn't know how or in what way. He felt his sickness ebb and the growth of new strength and wholeness within.

At last the healing fires subsided, and Corwin breathed out in a great sigh of relief. He let his head droop a moment and then looked up at Nia. She was smiling, her head drooping, too, but her face was a healthier color. "It's almost done," she said.

"Almost? What's left?" Corwin asked.

A name, the Farworlder prince thought back at him. *I need a name.*

"It's in the naming of things that our kind acknowledges the spirit in another being," Nia explained, "and then we are able to more readily join with it."

An idea instantly came to Corwin's mind. "We have a word, *gobaith*, that means hope. You said that this little one is the last hope of your people, so maybe that's what we should call him."

Corwin felt a glow of approval from the leviathan in the shell, and Nia smiled. "Yes," she said. "That's a very good name. Our prince takes the name given by the Avatar of the Land."

Nia bowed her head, still cupping the shell in her hands. She chanted words in an ancient language that Corwin couldn't understand, but through her mind and the prince's, he caught the sense of it—

King and Avatars, we are one
Minds and souls united ever
With this Name, let pain be done
in unity only Death may sever.
Gobaith, Gobaith, Gobaith.

Corwin could swear the Farworlder, Gobaith, made a sound like *wheeeee!* upon being given his new name.

Nia looked up again. "*Now* it's finished."

"Good," Corwin said, relieved. "Now we can—wait." He paused, listening closely. He was pretty sure he heard a faint clinking of metal beyond one of the kitchen doors. "Did you hear something?"

I have a bad feeling—Gobaith began.

Suddenly doors slammed open all around the kitchen, revealing men-at-arms with lances pointed and swords drawn. King Vortigern himself entered from the main door, followed by his three wizards. "So," the king said with narrowed eyes, "your witchery is complete. But what we want to know is, *what* have you done?"

It had been a trap. Corwin, Nia, and Gobaith had been too caught up in their magic to even see it coming.

"M-majesty," Corwin said, trying to recover from his shock, "we haven't done anything."

The wizards rolled their eyes. "Come, fellow, we aren't idiots," Anguis said. "We have watched here at the doors while you performed a spell of great magnitude. Persons within the castle have been behaving strangely, clearly by your design. Either you undo your treacherous spell, or you tell us how it was done so that we might undo it."

"If you are forthcoming about your treachery," King Vortigern said, "I may be moved to forego having you tortured and allow you a painless execution."

Nia straightened to stand her tallest. "Magi of this land," she began, "it wasn't a spell to bring harm. We were merely healing one another. If you were truly masters of your art, then you would know this."

The sorcerers glanced uncertainly at one another for a few moments. Finally, Anguis chuckled. "That's a very clever trick, young lady. But your arts may be subtle and deceptive to our eyes. You may have your work *appear* to be a healing spell, but we know otherwise from the effect it's having on the rest of the castle."

"Um, *what* effect on the rest of the castle?" Corwin asked, puzzled.

"Oh, I'm sure you'd like us to tell you just how successful your spell has been," King Vortigern sneered. "But I won't reward your curiosity. Just know that it didn't work as well as you'd hoped. After all, *we* are still awake and moving, and able to capture you."

Corwin looked at Nia and mouthed the words "Awake? Moving?"

Nia shrugged, clearly as baffled as he was.

"Majesty," said the wizard in the red robe and floppy hat, "before you . . . er . . . exact sentence, we should take possession of the shell, for clearly that is the focus of their power."

Corwin saw Anguis staring hungrily at the shell. *So it's not justice you're really after here*, Corwin thought. *You wanted to discover and steal the source of our power.*

King Vortigern wrinkled his nose, as if smelling something distasteful. "Very well. You, give that . . . thing up, and perhaps I will ensure that the blade of the headsman's axe is sharp."

Corwin looked again at Nia and he knew they shared the same thought. *If we give them Gobaith, all is lost.* He took a quick glance at all the doors. Three soldiers in each, a dozen in all. Plus the three wizards and the king. Well, the king wasn't likely to involve himself in any fracas. But still, the situation was hopeless.

How strange that we named the prince for hope, Corwin mused. *But as Fenwyck always said, when it's madness to hope, perhaps one's only hope lies in madness.* Corwin jumped up onto the table, holding the shell high. "You will not have our Talisman of Godlike Power!" he declared. "If you come near us, I shall smash it to the ground and its destruction will bring the castle down around our ears!"

Nia stared up at him, wide-eyed, but she didn't contradict him.

There was a long silence in the kitchen as every guard and wizard stared anxiously at the shell.

Finally Anguis grumbled, "It's another trick. Grab him."

But Corwin had now had time to examine the ceiling.

There was a niche where the great oak ceiling beams, round and thick as tree trunks, met the wall, and Corwin deftly tossed the shell into the niche. Two guards lunged for his legs. They were blown backward as Nia held out her hands and sent a blast of air at them. Two other guards lunged for her, and she rolled under the trestle table.

Corwin jumped up and shimmied along the ceiling beam, hoping to distract the guards from Nia. Even better, two sets of guards ran to the center of the room, colliding with one another.

The wizards were chanting noisily in one corner of the kitchen, next to the great hearth, and Corwin wondered if they could actually do real sorcery. He reached out and snatched the shell again, whispering into it, "Gobaith, can you stop whatever the sorcerers are doing?"

Black smoke rose out of the hearth fire and flowed over to the three wizards. They began to cough and choke in the acrid smoke, quite unable to speak. They stumbled away from the hearth, blundered blindly into another set of guards, and nearly knocked over the king.

"Good work," Corwin said. "Now what do we do?"

But Nia had the next idea. Under cover of the smoke, she crawled over to the hearth and grabbed a hooked iron bar from a rack. She then clambered back onto the trestle table. Using the iron bar, she reached out and snagged the lip of the cauldron on the fire and tipped it over. Scalding, steaming vegetable soup flooded the room.

The nearest guards screamed as the boiling broth soaked through their leather boots. King Vortigern and the wizards fled to the far end of the room. "Enough of this nonsense!" the king cried. "Grab them, or I'll have the whole lot of you thrown into the dungeons!"

Three guards, more afraid of the king than their scalded feet, ran to catch Nia on the table, as she was clearly the easier target. Or so they thought.

Nia beat their swords aside with the iron bar and then nimbly leaped to the side table where the bread dough lay. As one guard approached, she threw the dough in his face, where it stuck. He staggered back, knocking the other two guards to either side of him.

Meanwhile, another guard ran beneath Corwin and poked at him with his lance, trying to dislodge Corwin's arms from the beam.

"Be wary of the talisman," Anguis warned. "Don't damage the shell!"

"You should listen to him," Corwin said to the guard. Looking toward the main door, Corwin saw that, thanks to the smoke and the soup, there was a way clear—if the guards could be distracted. Corwin whispered into the shell, "Gobaith, can you fly? Go to your other Avatar, then." Corwin threw the shell to Nia.

Everyone in the room seemed to hold their breath as the shell sailed through the air. But Nia caught it deftly and held it up. "Here is the Talisman of Godlike Power!" she cried. "Who will dare take it from me?"

"Stupid girl," grumbled the guard nearest to her as he reached for her. Corwin wasn't sure exactly where Nia struck him with the iron bar but he screamed in a great deal of pain. The rest of the guards surged toward her, but the kitchen wasn't *that* big a room and all the guards rushing at once did more damage to one another than to Nia.

Quick as a spider, Corwin scuttled along the beam, dropping close to the door and hurrying out under cover of smoke. But Nia was still at the far end of the kitchen. Reluctantly revealing his location, Corwin cried, "Nia! To me!"

The wizards came boiling out of the room. "You bothersome cretin," Anguis growled. "You aren't carrying your precious talisman now—"

"Oh, shut up," Corwin growled back, and he sent a

blast of air, just as Nia would do, at the three wizards. It blew them back against the wall, knocking the wind out of them. He glanced back through the kitchen doorway. "Nia! Hurry!"

What he saw next amazed him. Holding the shell aloft, Nia seemed to run through the air, her feet bouncing off of helmets and lance points and, as a final insult, the head of the king himself. She landed gracefully beside Corwin. "Gobaith liked learning how to fly," she said. "But it has greatly weakened us."

"Then we shall have to fly on foot. C'mon," Corwin said, taking her arm.

They ran down the hallway, through the door, and down the stairs leading to the cistern. They heard the guards coming after them, not far behind, as they pounded down the first flight and then the second, and then discovered that the portcullis that had been up was now down.

Their way was blocked.

Corwin slammed into the portcullis but it didn't budge. He grabbed the bars and tried pushing it up, but it didn't move. He tried using his sorcerous powers to push the gate up, only to discover that Nia was right—they had been weakened, for any spell that one of them did drew upon the strengths of all three of them now. Corwin searched frantically for the drawing mechanism to raise the gate—

"You won't find it," said King Vortigern from the top of the nearest flight of stairs. "The winch is two floors up."

The guards flowed down the stairs, lance- and sword-points aimed straight for Corwin's and Nia's hearts.

"Well fought, I must say," the king went on. "Perhaps I will make it hours, not days, that you will be tortured. But really, you should have stayed in the exposure cage, you know. Your ends would have been far more merciful."

Corwin felt his heart pounding in his chest. He looked at Nia. *Can you blast them?* he thought at her.

Nia shook her head. "Too weak," she murmured.

The emboldened guards stepped closer and closer. But Corwin noticed there was still uncertainty and fear on their faces. *They don't know what we can still do*, he thought. *I have to try something . . . something that will drive them away.*

Fenwyck's voice echoed in his mind then. Words he had spoken long ago. *Always make things bigger, grander than they seem to be, lad. As outrageous as you can. People are far more willing to believe illusion than the truth.*

The most frightening thing Corwin had seen in recent

days was the kraken. Surely no one could be brave in the face of that horrible scarlet serpent.

"Beware!" Corwin cried. "As my last deed, with the last of my strength, I shall summon the kraken—a creature more terrifying than any you have ever known. It has a million mouths, which will devour you bit by bit. It has a scream that will curdle your blood!"

The guards paused for a long second.

"Oh, not again," grumbled one of the wizards from the back. "You've learned showmanship well from your Master Fenwyck's knee, lad, but we've heard enough of your blather. Just give up the shell."

Corwin looked at Nia and she nodded. She understood what he had to do. She put her hand on his arm and gave him what energy she could. Corwin bent over the shell, his eyes tightly closed. *Gobaith, this is what you must help me show*. He imagined with all his heart and memory what the kraken had looked like—the seawater turning red, the serpent rising from the waves, its great maw gaping. He imagined all the tiny sea creatures that made up its skin screaming at once in that horrible, sickening shriek.

Suddenly the stair passageway resounded with the powerful scream of the kraken, louder and more soulshaking for being in such a small space. Corwin's ears ached with the noise, and he trembled. The kraken's cry was soon followed by the screams of the guards and the wizards and the king, and the pounding of their feet as they all fled up the stairs.

Corwin heard the rumble of the portcullis as the gate opened behind him. Finally he dared open his eyes. The stairway was clear, except for the swords and lances dropped by the fleeing guards, and one of the wizards' soft leather shoes. "We did it," he said softly. He turned to Nia. "We did it!"

But she wasn't looking at him. She was staring behind him, wide-eyed with fear.

Corwin turned, slowly, afraid of what he would see. And there it was—the real kraken, rising out of the water of the cistern, its maw hanging open, great eyes staring, reeking of the sea. Swimming beside it were two dark-haired mermen and a full-grown Farworlder leviathan with glowing golden eyes.

Chapter Ten

Corwin's heart nearly stopped in his chest as the kraken towered higher, foul-smelling water dripping from between its fangs. "Did . . . did I . . . summon it?"

The older of the mermen came closer. "Don't think so highly of your powers, landling," he said with an accent much like Nia's. "You are only three, whereas I am multitudes."

"Ma'el," Nia said softly.

"So this is your evil king," Corwin said.

"Joab, the Farworlder you see there, is the king," Ma'el said smoothly. "I am his Avatar."

Corwin could see cold malevolence in the golden eyes of the Farworlder leviathan, and he could feel Gobaith's fear of Joab. "I don't understand—how can you speak my language so well?" Corwin blurted to Ma'el.

"My Atlantean spies have been visiting your land for years," Ma'el answered. "I have gained my knowledge through them, and through my newfound powers. But you must ignore Nia's words that Joab and I are evil. She's young. She doesn't understand how empires are won."

"With treachery and murder?" Nia demanded.

"Nearly always," Ma'el replied with a smile that seemed almost sad.

The other merman rose higher out of the water, and Corwin felt a jolt of recognition as he realized that this was the young man from Nia's painful memories.

"Nia," the merman purred, "it's wonderful to see you again."

Corwin could sense Nia's tumultuous feelings. "Who's he?" he asked.

"Cephan. A . . . former friend."

"Friend?" asked Cephan with a hurt frown. "Is that all you think we were? Do you always share kisses with your friends?"

Corwin felt his hands ball into fists, and he was about to launch himself into the water. But Nia put a calming hand on his arm. "He wants you to attack," she said softly. "He's taunting us."

"I, too, am happy to see you, dear Nia," Ma'el said, "because it means this ridiculous battle is over. I hope that you can finally understand that opposing me will only hurt you, along with your friend and the new Farworlder king. However, if you give the little fellow to me, we may all live in harmony and increase our powers together."

"Why would you let us live?" Corwin asked, as he eyed the kraken warily. The creature simply stared back at him, hunger in its eyes.

"Simple. Because I will have more power that way."

"You didn't let the other kings and Avatars live," Nia argued, the sadness in her voice again.

"Well, they weren't about to give me their . . . gifts willingly, were they? I had no choice but to take them by force. It leads to lesser quality, but the quantity makes up for it." Ma'el held out his arms, which were covered with strange bumps.

Nia gasped. "The oculae . . ."

Corwin could feel her disgust and horror wash over him. "What . . . what is . . ."

"Each of those bumps," Nia explained, "is the organ of magical power taken from a Farworlder. For every bump, a Farworlder was slaughtered."

Gobaith screamed with sorrow in his mind. Corwin closed his thoughts against the echoed pain. "Does Gobaith . . . have one?"

"Of course. So do I."

"You do?"

"Of course she does," said Ma'el. "I gave it to her as a birthday present when she was very, very young. That is why she's as skilled as she is."

"I was your experiment," Nia growled.

"Don't take it personally," Ma'el said. "You were only one of many. As for you." Ma'el turned his gaze to Corwin. "You are a rather interesting case yourself. It would appear your Gobaith got somewhat lucky. Should I call you a landling or . . . something else?"

"What are you talking about?" Corwin demanded, his face flushing.

"Ah. You are unaware of your parentage. Never mind. I expect it will likely not matter."

"My parentage?" Corwin's body tensed up. "What do you know about my family?"

"Corwin!" Nia said, squeezing his arm. "Don't let him bait you."

"Bait?" Ma'el echoed, with mock hurt pride. "I was able to give you proper information on *your* father, Nia, wasn't I?"

"What do you know? Who is my father?" Corwin yelled, barely able to restrain himself from lunging at the mermyd.

"Well, it certainly isn't me," Ma'el said. "And you

aren't in much of a position to make rude demands. You see, if you decide to turn down my generous offer, I *will* have to destroy you three. And whether you believe it or not, I really don't want to. But I must do what's necessary for the good of Atlantis."

Corwin felt as if he could explode. He had just done all he could to drive away one madman, and now he was faced with another. He tried to reach Gobaith's mind. *What can we do?*

Do not surrender, was all Gobaith would send back.

"I know what you're thinking, young fellow," Ma'el said, "for my power is tenfold greater than yours, and I can perceive the unis in its entirety. You know the speed of my helpful assistant here." He indicated the kraken beside him. "You can't possibly escape. And while your sorcery is impressive for a new Avatar, you have expended most of your energy. You're young. Why waste such promising lives?"

"Indeed," Cephan chimed in, gazing at Nia in a way that made Corwin's blood boil. "I would be heartbroken, Nia, if Ma'el were forced to hurt you. The loss of such beauty, intelligence, and talent would be a criminal waste. My offer to you is still open. Let us rule Atlantis together." He held out his hand to her.

"You murdered my cousin," Nia replied coldly. "You helped Ma'el murder the rest of my family. Do you think I would ever want to be by your side? I would rather die."

Ma'el's mocking expression grew serious. "I'm sorry, Nia, but that's your only other choice."

What can I do, what can I do? Corwin thought. *The only thing the kraken fears is the sun, and there is no sunlight here. If only I still had the burning glass . . . no, it wouldn't help. But would an illusion of the burning glass and its sunlight work?* Desperate for any solution, Corwin thought at Gobaith, *Give me what power you can.*

Corwin raised his hand, forming a circle with his fingers. Closing his eyes tight, he imagined the light of the sun coursing through the circle, focused into a tight beam. He opened his eyes again and saw a bright ray streaming from his hand, spearing the kraken in the neck. The creature screamed, a shriek more horrible than any it had made before. Nia crouched and covered her ears, and Corwin wished he could do so as well.

But the spell worked. The kraken disintegrated and fell into the water as if melting.

"Well, that was rather imaginative," Ma'el said, his eyes slightly widened in surprise, but obviously not very perturbed. "You realize that I could summon the creature again at will, and that you've already pushed your poor Farworlder king to his limits. But the kraken probably isn't even necessary. I have other, easier means."

Joab surged forward to the steps and whipped his tentacles around Nia's ankles. As she shrieked, he dragged her toward the water.

"Nia!" Corwin cried.

"Run!" Nia called back. "They have tails, not legs like me. They can't chase you. Take Gobaith away. Run!"

But Ma'el swam up to the base of the stairs, a smug smile on his bearded face. He flopped up onto the lowermost dry steps, revealing from the waist down a powerful fishtail covered with black scales. Then, to Corwin's horror, the tail began to ripple and shudder. A split ran up from the end fin, dividing the tail in two, as Ma'el uttered a loud but triumphant cry of pain. The scales receded, and muscles differentiated. Instead of a tail, Ma'el was now forming two legs, as a land-dweller would have. Soon he was able to stand on his own new feet.

Corwin backed up a step, but how could he leave when Nia was being held captive?

Ma'el smiled. "Come here, Joab. You're distressing Nia's friend."

Joab released Nia to Cephan's imprisoning embrace

and surged toward the steps. But instead of stopping at the water's edge, the Farworlder slithered onto the steps. It was bigger than the leviathan Corwin had seen on the beach. And a bit older. And a mottled dark purple in color. To see such a large version of a Farworlder, with such malice in its eyes, crawling toward him made Corwin's blood run cold and his legs freeze in fear. *How fast can one of those move on land?* Corwin wondered.

But Joab did not come after Corwin. The Farworlder instead went to Ma'el. It reached up with its tentacles and wrapped them around Ma'el's waist. And then it slithered up Ma'el's legs and back. As Corwin watched in horror, Joab settled himself on Ma'el's shoulders, his great, bulbous head looming behind that of the merman. Joab wrapped a tentacle around each of Ma'el's thick, muscled arms, and two tentacles around his chest. This left six long, slimy tentacles to wave menacingly toward Corwin. Together, Ma'el and Joab formed a two-headed, twelve-armed monster. Corwin's mouth went dry as he stared at the terrifying new creature facing him, and his legs remained glued to the ground.

Ma'el/Joab began to walk up the steps toward Corwin. "Did you really think destroying my sea serpent would help you?"

"Corwin, *run!*" Nia cried again.

Finally Corwin regained control of his muscles. Cradling the shell tightly in his arms, he dashed up the stairs as fast as he could go. *Cephan won't kill her. They want our power. She'll be all right,* he kept telling himself, wishing he could believe it. It was just like Fenwyck all over again. *But Fenwyck gave his life to save mine. If Nia loses hers, I die, too.*

Corwin pounded through the door at the top of the stairs and slammed it shut behind him. He dashed down the hall past the kitchens and entered a large meeting hall filled with wooden benches. There were men here, dressed like well-to-do merchants, but as King Vortigern had said, they appeared to be sleeping, snoring loudly. *Aha,* Corwin realized, as it all fit together in his mind. *I'll bet the spell the wizards blamed on us was Ma'el's work.*

Corwin slammed the door to this room shut and piled as many benches against it as he could in ten seconds. To his surprise and dismay, none of the men in the room awakened. Corwin shook the shoulder of one of them. But when the pounding began on the other side of the door, Corwin ran.

He found a door that led into a courtyard on the north side of the castle. He was shocked to discover that it was later in the day than he'd expected. The sun was setting. Corwin didn't have much time to decide where to run, and some instinct told him to run upward, that Ma'el/Joab might tire if they had many stairs to climb, if they weren't used to dry land.

Before him, beside the northwest wall of the castle, stood the unfinished tower that had given King Vortigern so many troubles. But it was somewhat higher than the castle wall itself, so Corwin headed for it. He slipped into a narrow rectangular entryway and dashed up the stairs within.

Around and around, in dizzying circles, up the cracked, broken, twisted stairs, Corwin ran. He finally emerged at the landing that was presently the top of the tower. Corwin leaned against the broken stone of the tower wall and gasped for breath. Looking out over the castle, he saw no sign of Ma'el/Joab. *Maybe I lost them,* he thought hopefully. *Or maybe they returned to deal with Nia.* He shuddered, trying not to think about that.

The tower loomed over the River Twy, far below to the west. The sun had sunk just below the trees beyond the river. To the north, a road wound away toward the eastern plains. Corwin spotted several horsemen riding away down the road, hellbent-for-leather. It was King

Vortigern, his son, Prince Vortimer, and the three wizards.

"And good riddance to you," Corwin muttered, watching them go. "If Ma'el does conquer your kingdom, it will be no less than you deserve."

Corwin felt a chill slither down his spine, and he turned around, then gasped. Ma'el/Joab stood there right in front of him, the tentacles around Ma'el's chest writhing, reaching for Corwin. The oculae beneath the skin of Ma'el's arms pulsed like little hearts.

"What, did you think we weren't capable of stealth?" the creature mocked. "You are right, however. When we conquer the land kingdoms, it will be no less than you all deserve."

Corwin tried to run to the archway above the stairs, but Ma'el/Joab blocked it.

"What will it take to convince you," Ma'el/Joab went on, "that this entire exercise is futile? Other than impressing me with your skills, you have only drained yourself and your Farworlder of much-needed energy."

"Nia has shown me what you did to her city," Corwin retorted. "I had to do what I could to stop you."

"But you see, that's the point," said Ma'el/Joab, coming toward him. "You can't stop me. No one can. Just give me little Gobaith, and we will all return to the sea and be happy." The great, dark, bulbous head of Joab throbbed and flowed over Ma'el's head to form a giant hood, the golden eyes to either side of Ma'el's ears. Corwin hadn't thought he would ever see anything more horrible than the kraken had been, but he was beginning to change his mind.

"I would drown in the sea," Corwin said, backing up against the wall.

"Not necessarily. A curious thing happens to those who stop breathing in very cold water. Their revival becomes . . . more likely, if dealt with in time. And should you survive the journey, Atlantis has some air-filled dry rooms where we could sequester you . . . for a while." Ma'el/Joab paused, then continued. "You might not enjoy it, but at least your life wouldn't end here and now. And you also might discover some interesting things about yourself. . . . Maybe it wouldn't be as difficult for you to survive in water as you think," he added in the same cryptic tone he'd used earlier, when he'd mentioned Corwin's background.

Corwin opened his mouth to question him further, but then remembered what Nia had warned. "I won't listen to anything you say," he said as defiantly as he could. "And I won't let you win," he said, desperately trying to think of what to do. Gobaith was shivering in his shell, also attempting something, but Corwin couldn't tell what.

"As you wish," said Ma'el/Joab. The purple tentacles lashed out toward Corwin as the merman/leviathan rushed at him, pressing him against the broken, crenellated wall. Corwin was able to hold the shell containing Gobaith just out of reach for a few moments. Then one of Joab's tentacles managed to wrap itself around his wrist.

Time seemed to slow down, seconds stretching long as Corwin considered what his last act might be. Looking over his shoulder, he could see the River Twy far below. "I wonder, Ma'el, with all your powers, can you fly?" he asked, tossing the silvery shell over the side of the tower.

Ma'el/Joab roared words Corwin couldn't comprehend and stretched out over the edge of the wall, reaching out arms and tentacles to catch the shell.

Corwin watched as the glimmering shell arced outward. *If it strikes the water, Gobaith might just live.*

But the sun had dipped below the horizon. To Corwin's horror, the Twy ran red and suddenly a column of scarlet water shot out of the river. Ma'el had again summoned the kraken. The creature's mouth gaped wide to receive the falling shell. . . .

"Noooo!" cried Corwin.

"Skraaaaaw!" came a cry from the forest. Nag flew out of the trees beside the river. Diving between the kraken's jaws, the raven snatched Gobaith's shell out of the air. The kraken's fangs closed on nothing, and the creature screamed in frustration.

Corwin pounded the wall with his fist in astonished joy. "Good Nag! Good bird! I'll never call you useless again!"

Carrying the hope of Atlantis, the raven flew back among the treetops, disappearing into the shadowed canopy of the forest.

Chapter Eleven

Ma'el/Joab roared again, this time a great cry of frustration. Joab's tentacles slid around Corwin's neck and tightened. Corwin could smell the reek of dead fish from the Farworlder, as well as Ma'el's breath. "You idiot!" Ma'el cried. "Dry-lander kingdoms have never been able to crush Atlantis's power. Nor will you succeed this time! You will die, and the last king and Avatar will die with you. Only I will remain, and I *will* conquer all!"

Corwin knew his neck could be snapped at any second. Time slowed again, and Corwin could see in precise detail the veins on Ma'el's arms, and the strange oculae lumps throbbing beneath the merman's skin. *They look so delicate—I wonder if they can be harmed? Well, I don't have anything left to lose. Why not find out?*

Corwin lashed out and struck one of the lumps with his fist.

Ma'el/Joab screamed. A bolt of pain, like lightning,

speared through Corwin's mind. But Joab's stranglehold loosened for just a moment.

Corwin struck again, a different lump. Again Ma'el/Joab wailed, and Corwin's mind howled with pain. He used the pain to drive himself on, striking on lump after lump on Ma'el's arms.

How strange, Corwin thought through his psychic agony, *that Ma'el's greatest strength can become his weakness. If it's this painful for me, how much worse it must be for him.*

A blackness enveloped them that wasn't natural. *What is this?* Corwin wondered blindly. *Some new terror that Ma'el can summon at will?*

Ghosts and demons danced in the shadows. *Can he drag the very shades out of Hades?* Not knowing what else to do, Corwin continued to seek each oculus under Ma'el's skin and strike it as hard as he could.

Another roar from Ma'el/Joab, and the heads of many kraken screamed around them—the tower roof was swarming with them.

Sharks and giant eels of the deep rushed at Corwin with fanged jaws wide, and he braced himself for the pain, but they didn't bite. With a shake, he continued to beat at the oculae, fighting through the fear. Then one shark actually swam right through him. *Why aren't I dead?* Corwin marveled. *Why aren't the kraken shredding me to pieces?* Then suddenly it all made sense. Corwin almost laughed as he realized that this was all an illusion created by Ma'el/Joab. He shut his eyes and continued punching.

Joab's tentacles slithered around him, pinning Corwin's arms to his side. Corwin opened his eyes. The illusions were gone. Ma'el, his face contorted in a mask of rage, tried to punch Corwin in the face, but Joab was holding him too close for the blow to have power. Corwin lunged to the side. Pressing his face against Ma'el's right upper arm, he fixed his teeth around an oculus lump and bit down as hard as he could. The taste of blood and bile and sea brine filled his mouth.

Ma'el roared again; then his grip slipped away and he fell to the flagstones. Joab's tentacles writhed in the air and Ma'el shuddered all over. The muscles in his legs rippled, and black scales flowed over the skin. A black pool of ink spread out from beneath them like blood.

He's no longer controlling his body, Corwin realized. Seizing his chance, Corwin grabbed Ma'el's ankles and pulled him next to the wall. Ma'el and Joab tried to hit Corwin with fist and tentacle, but instead their limbs flailed helplessly. Gripping one of Ma'el's wrists, Corwin hauled him and Joab up and slung them onto the rim of the wall. With one mighty shove, Corwin lifted Ma'el by the legs and shoved both him and the leviathan Joab over the side of the tower.

Corwin watched as merman and leviathan fell down and down. They struck the rocks at the base of the castle with a loud *whump* and then rolled down the embankment, stopping at the river's edge.

Good, thought Corwin, gasping from the exertion. *He didn't reach the water, so he won't be able to heal. With luck, tomorrow's sun will bleach his bones like those of a beached fish.*

One of Ma'el's hands twitched. To Corwin's shock, the river turned red again, and a kraken—though a much smaller kraken than before—rose out of the water. It slithered up the embankment and wrapped itself almost tenderly around Ma'el's tail. Its myriad tiny mouths were keening as if in sorrow. It pulled Ma'el and Joab into the river, where they sank below the surface and vanished.

Corwin stared at the river for long, long minutes, listening to his ragged breathing, feeling his heart still pounding in his chest, waiting for Ma'el or Joab or the kraken to resurface. But they didn't.

Is it done, then? Corwin wondered in amazement. *Are they dead? Are Gobaith and I and Nia all safe now?* And then he remembered . . . *Nia! Cephan still has her!*

Staggering from his ordeal, Corwin stumbled to the doorway. Struggling to keep his balance and not fall down the stairs, he slid his right side against the wall so that he wouldn't tumble. He didn't even care about the stone scraping against his skin.

At the bottom of the tower stairs, the courtyard seemed impossibly wide. Not knowing quite where he was finding the strength, Corwin staggered across it to the meeting room door. Fortunately, Ma'el/Joab had been kind enough to smash it open, so Corwin didn't have to tug on a heavy door. The inner door, likewise, had been pulverized to splinters, and the benches Corwin had piled against it were scattered like sticks. The men in the room were still curled up on the floor, asleep. Corwin deeply envied them.

He staggered down the hallway, past the kitchens, aware that something was tugging at his mind. He had forgotten . . . something. Or needed something. But he could only focus on the thought of Nia in danger, and that kept his legs moving, kept him putting one foot after another.

He reached the stairs down to the cistern and again he slid against the slimy stone, staggering downward. He heard a voice—Cephan's voice, he realized—speaking in a language he didn't understand.

Corwin came around the last landing and saw at the bottom of the stairs, just above the waterline, Cephan bending over Nia. There was a dagger in the merman's hand, pointed at Nia's forehead. Corwin stepped forward but tripped over a fallen lance on the stairs and fell forward. He belly-flopped on the stairs, his hands slapping down on a dropped sword. The blade left shallow cuts in his palms.

Cephan tilted his head. There was a mad cast to his bright blue eyes and a strange smile on his handsome features. "Look who's joined us, Nia," he said. "It's your new friend. He's the one who sent us the pain. He's the one who has drained all your strength. You should hate him. But you can't feel anything now, can you, precious Nia? So you won't feel it when I take your oculus from you. If Ma'el is dead, and you die, I can at last become master of Atlantis." He bent over her again.

Corwin's right hand found the hilt of the sword beneath him. He managed to roll over, putting his back to the wall. *This is what I was missing . . . a weapon.* But though he could grasp it, he knew his forearms were too weary to wield the sword with any power.

"I'm not afraid of you, land-boy," Cephan said, drawing a line across Nia's forehead with the point of the dagger. "I'm much stronger than you."

Corwin wasn't even paying attention to what the merman was saying. His eyes were full of Nia, lying helpless on the stairs, the dagger poised between her eyes. Corwin slid farther down the stone steps on his bottom, ignoring the pain.

"Don't come any closer!" Cephan warned. "This is a delicate operation. If I slip, she'll die."

"She'll die no matter what, won't she?" Corwin asked. "But you don't want the oculus damaged. It wouldn't be any use to you then. If you slip, you might ruin your chance to rule."

Cephan turned his head, wearing a nasty smile. "What do you care? No matter what happens, you're already dead."

"Yes," said Corwin. He stood, pressing his back against the wall. His legs shook with fatigue. "The dead have no cares, do they? The dead can do anything."

A sudden glint of fear appeared in Cephan's eyes. He pointed his dagger at Corwin. "Stay back! Or I'll—"

"You'll what?" asked Corwin. "Kill me?"

Cephan held the dagger out even farther. Corwin realized that this was what he had been waiting for. With no exertion at all, he pointed the sword toward Cephan's back. And fell on top of him.

Cephan grunted, and his body shuddered beneath Corwin. Corwin rolled farther down the steps, his arm striking the water of the cistern. He looked back up at Cephan.

The mermyd was gasping, lying on top of Nia, blood dripping from his mouth. Corwin's eyes darted to the sword—judging from the length of the remainder of the blade sticking out from Cephan's back, it shouldn't have gone into Nia as well. *And I'm still alive*, Corwin thought. *So Nia must be as well. I think.*

Cephan pushed himself up on his arms. Coughing, the mermyd turned, and Corwin knew what he was doing. *He wants to get to the water, where he might heal.*

Cephan slid down the two steps between him and Corwin. *No you don't*, thought Corwin, and he raised his arm and bent his knee to make himself into an obstacle. It worked—Cephan slid into him and stopped on the lowermost stair with a final groan. But his impact pushed Corwin into the water.

It was all right, really, Corwin told himself. The cool water felt wonderful on his exhausted body. He wished he could float there forever, gazing on Nia's face. It would end now, and he was sorry his death would also kill Nia and Gobaith. But they had stopped Ma'el, hadn't they? And outfoxed King Vortigern. These were things to be proud of, to take into the afterlife. Whether he faced the Catholic Heaven, or the Hall of Heroes, or Mount Olympus, surely his deeds would have earned him a place, outweighing all his sins.

Corwin felt himself sinking, the chill water flowing over his face. He didn't mind. To sleep in water was a better fate than Fenwyck had met. Bidding the world, especially Nia, good-bye, he watched the glimmering light on the surface recede above him, and he slipped into darkness.

He awoke again suddenly, with a sharp stinging on his cheeks. He coughed, and water flowed out of his mouth.

"Corwin! Corwin!" Nia shouted above him.

Corwin opened his eyes. Nia's face hovered over him, and she was grinning through her tears. "Corwin! You . . . you're alive, and you're safe!"

Corwin tried to speak and coughed up water again. He

rolled over and let his lungs and stomach heave more water out until he could breathe smoothly again. Glancing around, he saw that he was back on the stairs beside the underground cistern. "You're right. I'm uncomfortable and in pain and I'm wet. I must be alive. But . . . how?"

"Gobaith saved you. I don't know how. He's stronger now, so he must have found water. He woke me and told me to find you. I was so afraid. . . ." Nia blushed and looked away. "I wasn't thinking clearly."

Corwin felt a warm glow inside. He ran a finger over her cheek, brushing the remnants of her tears away.

Nia smiled shyly and sat back. "Still. Now we have to think of what to do next. What happened to Ma'el and Joab?"

"What about Cephan? Is he . . ."

Nia pressed her lips together, then turned and pointed out over the cistern.

Corwin saw Cephan's body draped over a low pile of rubble, a fallen column, just above the water.

"He won't rise again," Nia said. "I made sure." There was an emptiness behind her eyes, and Corwin knew it couldn't have been easy to do such a thing to a former love, even after the way he'd betrayed her. "Is Ma'el dead as well?" she asked.

"I don't know," Corwin said with a frown. "I distracted him by hitting the bumps on his arms and then threw him and Joab off the tower. They struck the ground, and I thought they'd die. But the kraken came out of the river and pulled them into the water."

Nia's brow furrowed. "That's not good. With his great powers, he could easily revive. Healing is one of an Avatar's best skills, and Ma'el has the power of ten Avatars. And grown Farworlders can be difficult to kill."

Corwin groaned and lay back. "And here I thought it was all over. Nia, what are we going to do? I can't fight anymore."

Nia reached over and squeezed his shoulder. "He won't threaten us for a while. If Ma'el and Joab live, they will need to go back to the great ocean. We mermyds can't stay out of the sea for too long, nor can Farworlders."

Corwin looked at Nia. "That means you, too."

Nia glanced down at her hands. "Yes."

Corwin sighed. "Well, then. Our first goal is leaving this accursed castle. Followed by getting you back to the ocean."

"And we must find Gobaith," Nia added.

"Is he in trouble?"

"No, not yet. But until we know where he is, we can't

be sure trouble won't find him. Also, it's good for Avatars and their king to be near one another. It brings greater comfort and . . ." She waved her hands as she searched for the words. " . . . sharing of minds."

"We don't have a word for that in my language," Corwin said.

"Perhaps someday you will," Nia said with a sad smile.

Corwin sighed and stood up. To his surprise, he felt stronger and clearheaded, though not completely back to health. He held out his hand to Nia and helped her up. "Should we swim back out?"

Nia shook her head, staring out at the black water of the cistern. "If Ma'el is still alive, he might have his creature lying in wait for us. It's safer to leave by land."

"Good point," Corwin agreed. "Let's go."

Together they walked through the castle. What few servants and nobles they saw were still sleeping soundly. "How is it," asked Corwin, "that these people still sleep under Ma'el's magic when Ma'el himself has been hurt? Wouldn't that break the spell?"

Nia shrugged. "It depends on the magic he used. If he simply called upon the normal sleeping urge in their bodies, they might sleep the usual amount they would in a night."

"This magic stuff is more complicated than I thought," Corwin said.

"Much more, I'm sure," Nia said, smiling.

As they passed by a nobleman in fine silks, Corwin stopped and peered at the man closely. It was Lord Faustus. Corwin deftly removed the man's coin purse from his belt.

"What are you doing?" Nia asked, astonished. "Isn't that theft? Isn't that wrong in your land?"

"My guardian, Fenwyck, used to say, 'Wherever you go in life, always take something.' This man nearly cost us our lives. He won't be in any trouble without the money—if nothing else, he can sell his clothes. We, on the other hand, have dire need of this, and we aren't likely to get it elsewhere. Besides, we've just saved the kingdom. We're entitled to a little reward, aren't we?"

"If you say so," Nia replied. "But I'm still not used to your ways. They're more complicated than I thought."

"Much more, I'm sure," Corwin responded with another smile.

As they continued down the corridor, they came upon a scullery maid curled up beside her mop and bucket. When they passed, she suddenly shifted and yawned.

"Well, I guess that answers my question about the spell," said Corwin. "Maybe we'd better hurry."

They went out to the courtyard, now illuminated only by the dim glow of twilight. The evening was delightfully warm, and crickets sang in the shadows.

"I'm so tired," Nia sighed. "The air is so dry. Will we have to walk far, do you think?"

"I had another idea, actually," Corwin said. "The stables should be this way, from the smell of things."

"Stables?"

"Remember those large four-legged animals you saw when you first met me?"

"Oh. Yes?" Nia sounded a little uncertain.

"They're called horses. And we're going to ride one out of here."

Nia's eyes went wide. "Like those men did when I chased them away from you. Those creatures . . . go very fast."

"Not necessarily. You can keep a horse at a walk with no trouble. I suppose you don't have any creatures you ride where you come from."

"Yes, we do. But they're slow. You would call them . . . sea turtles."

"Ah. Yes. That would explain why horses might frighten you. Well, I'll try to find a gentle one."

As they came to the enclosure where the royal horses

were kept, Corwin saw a stable hand hanging up a lantern and yawning.

"What now?" Nia whispered.

"As my former guardian said, people will readily believe illusion. Leave it to me." Corwin stepped forward, but stayed in shadow. Speaking in imitation of the voice of Prince Vortimer, Corwin declared, "What is this, man? Sleeping on the job? I should report you to my father!"

The poor young fellow nearly dropped the lantern. "Y-your Highness?" He bowed his head and tugged at his forelock. "Forgive me, Highness. I was only resting. I couldn't help myself. It's this heat. Please don't tell the king. I will work twice as long tonight. Please. I have elderly parents who depend upon my pay——"

"Silence!" Corwin roared, though he truly felt sorry for the fellow. "I'm in a hurry, so I might punish you only a little bit for your transgression."

"Oh, thank you, thank you——"

"DID I NOT FORBID YOU TO SPEAK?"

The boy whimpered but said nothing.

"Now," Corwin continued, "first you will face the wall and kneel. Close your eyes and think of ways you may better serve the Crown."

The boy spun around and knelt before the wall, as instructed.

"Next you will tell me which horse you have currently saddled and ready that is the most gentle, for I have a lady with me who is in ill health and needs to see a healer."

The boy was silent.

"Oh. You may speak now," Corwin added.

"M'lord, a party must have left earlier, for several of the horses . . . um . . ."

Oh, he's afraid to say more, Corwin thought, *because the king must have fled with the best steeds. I'd better reassure him or he'll die of fear*. "Yes, yes," Corwin said. "My father took a hunting party out earlier this evening. While you were sleeping. A good thing they didn't see you. What's left?"

"There is . . . Meadowflower, Highness." The boy cringed as if expecting to be beaten.

"Which one is that?"

The boy paused. "Highness, that's the horse you rode from boyhood. Or so you yourself told me."

Uh-oh. "I KNOW THAT!" Corwin declared. "I was testing your memory. Where is she?"

The boy pointed with a shaking hand. "*He* . . . is that way, Highness."

"Quite right. Stay where you are and pray that the king is of forgiving mind when he returns from hunting." Taking Nia's hand, Corwin whispered, "C'mon."

"I don't think he believed you."

"It doesn't matter, as long as his disbelief takes a while to sink in."

They found at the end of the stables an old gray gelding with a long, shaggy mane, munching on hay. The horse looked up at them with complete calm, as if he'd seen everything. "Well, I expect this one should be gentle," Corwin said.

"What do I do?" Nia asked.

"You get on its back." Corwin was about to put his hands on Nia's waist to lift her; in fact, he was looking forward to it.

"Oh, I see. This is a step," she said before he had the chance. She put her left foot in the stirrup and swung her leg over, as though she were a born rider. "Is this right?"

"I must remember never to underestimate your intelligence," Corwin said. "That was perfect. Now scoot back so I can sit ahead of you."

Corwin untied the reins from a nearby post and mounted the horse as well. He hadn't ridden much . . . horse thieving was a hanging offense, and Fenwyck had never been able to afford one. But he had seen enough to know how it was done. "Now put your arms around me and hold on tight," Corwin said, "in case the horse takes off quickly." *Which this horse is not likely to do*, he added to himself.

Nia did so and Corwin smiled as she rested against his back. He picked up the rein loop and said, "Ho, Meadowflower. Get up. Let's move."

The horse looked up at him, still chewing.

Corwin shook the reins. "Come on. Let's go."

The horse turned its head back to the hay trough and grabbed another mouthful.

"Corwin . . ." Nia tapped his shoulder.

The stable boy was standing beside the post. "You aren't Prince Vortimer," he growled.

"And you should be very glad that I'm not," Corwin pointed out, "considering your inexcusable behavior. Here." On impulse, Corwin took Faustus's money bag from his pocket and tossed it to the boy. "You make a terrible stable hand. Go find some other employment. Maybe as a squire."

The boy looked in the bag and his eyes nearly popped out of his head. "Thank you, sir! You're an angel, sir! The prince shall hear nothing of this from me, sir!"

"Good. Now we'll just be on our way. Assuming the horse is willing."

"Oh," said the boy. "You must tell him, 'To the hilt, Meadowflower!' That's what His Highness always said."

"Very well. Thank you. Ahem." Feeling silly, Corwin again imitated Vortimer. "To the hilt, Meadowflower!"

The horse sighed a heavy, patient sigh and turned. He clopped nonchalantly out of the stables and toward the castle gate without any steering at all from Corwin.

"You're right," Nia said. "This beast isn't too fast at all."

"Truly, in fact I think this may be his top speed."

But as they approached the gate, Corwin saw those guards were awake and none too happy to see a stranger.

"Halt. The gate is closed to all travel until sunrise."

Corwin was out of clever ideas.

The stable boy came running up alongside. "Uncle Morcar! It is I, Gowan. This man is on a special duty from His Highness Prince Vortimer himself. He escorts an ill lady who must seek medicine at once. I am to go with them, to guide them. Please let us out. You know how wrathful His Highness can be when his orders aren't followed at once."

Uncle Morcar rolled his eyes. "God spare me from the whims of princes. Very well. Bide a moment." He conferred with the other guard and they slid open the bar across the double gate. The guards pushed the doors open just enough to make a passage big enough for the horse to pass through. "Hurry along, if you will, good sir," Morcar said to Corwin. "May the lady regain her health soon. As for you, Gowan, go on home as soon as you're done with your errand. You know your mother worries when you stay out long o'nights."

"Yes, Uncle. I will, Uncle."

Corwin nodded regally to the guards and allowed the boy to lead Meadowflower through the gate as if it were the most natural thing in the world to be doing.

As soon as they were across the drawbridge and on the main road into town, Gowan said, "I will leave you now, sir, m'lady, but may angels guide you on your journey, wherever you are going!" He ran off into the night laughing and jumping for joy.

"Thus is charity rewarded," said Corwin, with some irony.

"It was very kind of you," Nia said, "but I thought you said we needed those coins."

"And we did, didn't we? It bought us our way out. Besides, now should Lord Faustus ever question me as to whether I have his purse, I can in all honesty say no."

Nia sighed, laughing. "I don't think I will *ever* understand your land-dweller ways."

"Perhaps just as well. Ho, to the hilt, Meadowflower!" The horse lurched forward and plodded down the road.

A full yellow moon was rising in the west. Stars were shining overhead. It was really a very pleasant night. Except for one problem. "Where should we look for Gobaith?" Corwin asked. "I haven't felt a trace of his mind since I threw him off the tower. Can you sense his surroundings at all?"

"I feel sick when I try," Nia said.

Corwin found that odd, so he reached out for Gobaith's thoughts as well. And the world spun around him, vertigo so strong that he nearly fell off the horse.

"Corwin! Are you all right?"

"I see what you mean," Corwin said, shutting off that part of his thoughts at once and clinging to the front of the saddle. "But where could he possibly be to feel like that? Where would that crazy bird have taken him?"

"Rawwwk!" the cry came from overhead.

"Nag?"

There was a *plop*, and something wet splashed into Corwin's lap. "Hey!" He grabbed it—it was the shell, which was full of seawater. Gobaith's tentacles flopped outside the lip of the shell and curled gratefully around Corwin's fingers.

"So that's where he's been, and why he's been dizzy!" Nia said. "Gobaith likes to fly, but not when carried by a wild raven."

Nag landed on Corwin's shoulder and laughed and laughed and laughed.

Corwin and Nia couldn't help but join in.

Epilogue

Late summer sunlight sparkled off the ripples in Carmarthen Bay. Corwin sat on the rocky shore watching Nia and Gobaith play in the water. It had been two weeks since their escape from the castle, and Nia was completely back to health. Gobaith was now nearly four feet long, and his skin had turned an iridescent blue-green. He hadn't lost his enjoyment of flying and would sometimes launch himself out of the bay and skim over the water for yards at a time before diving back in. It was rather eerie to watch him and Nag race each other over the waves. Corwin could only wonder what passing fishermen might think.

Corwin had gradually realized that the Farworlder had . . . well, a personality, even more complicated than his own. Gobaith had a sense of humor, a wisdom far surpassing his age and experience, and an uncanny sense of the unis, the fabric of space and time that binds all things. Having come to know Gobaith had given Corwin greater understanding of the world around him, and Corwin knew he would have been much worse off had he never met the Farworlder. He actually *liked* the little squid.

Nia was also a complicated matter. Through her, he now saw the fair sex in a much different light. Unlike most young men of his land, he now saw her in much the same way as he saw Gobaith—as a full person, with feelings and thoughts much like his own, but also unexpectedly opposite at times. And he liked her more and more every day. But he couldn't help remembering what old Henwyneb had told him—how no good ever came from the union of a mermyd with a land-dweller. . . .

Nia popped up in the water a few feet away, brushing the water back from her face and smoothing her silvery hair with her hands. Beside her, Gobaith allowed his head to bob out of the water, like a green fisherman's float with eyes. Nia was wearing a mischievous smile, and Corwin could tell she was working to hide her thoughts from him.

"Have a good swim?" Corwin asked, waiting to hear what the joke was.

"Yes, though Gobaith always tries to wear me out. He's still young in spirit, but he's becoming so strong. I can't keep up with him."

"Well, he'll keep you in better shape for those races you've told me you have down in Atlantis."

Nia glanced away and her smile vanished.

Corwin mentally kicked himself. He should have known better than to mention Atlantis. He knew she worried about her people. Corwin felt a familiar growing fear that she would be leaving him someday soon.

But her mysterious smile returned. "Gobaith has been telling me secrets."

"What? Telling you and not me? That isn't fair, is it?"

"He wasn't sure you were ready. But I think you are. So I'll tell you."

"Ready for what? Tell me what?"

"Remember those strange hints Ma'el made, about knowing something about your past and who you really are?"

"How could I forget?" Corwin growled. "Him teasing me like that. I'm glad I gave him every blow I could."

"Ma'el wasn't just teasing," Nia said. "I'm sorry, I was wrong. He actually knew something. Gobaith has been watching you and has figured it out. I should have seen it myself."

"Now you're being as bad as Ma'el!" Corwin shouted. "What is it that you know?"

"That your father must have been a mermyd, Corwin. Your . . . form is mostly that of a land-dweller; you take after your human mother more. But you have mermyd blood within you, which is why you swim so easily underwater."

"A merman! Me?" Corwin almost laughed. He knew by now how wise Gobaith was, but the Farworlder was way off on this one. "But I'm a clumsy oaf in water!"

"Has anyone ever taught you how to swim?"

Corwin thought back. "Not that I can remember."

"But you knew how, anyway. You simply haven't had much practice until recently."

"But I—I mean, I don't even have gills!" he blurted, thinking of the most obvious flaw in this far-fetched concept.

"You have the . . . structure for them. Under your skin."

Corwin put his hands to the sides of his neck. He felt ridges there, but he had always thought those were muscles. "Gobaith," Corwin shouted out to the floating Farworlder, "is this really true?"

It is so, Gobaith replied in his thoughts. *You have mermyd blood. This is why you survived receiving my mark and my toxin. It was very fortunate that I found you. Or you found me.*

"Maybe it wasn't luck," Nia said. "Maybe Ar'an, as the last magic of his life, searched the unis for one who could bear your mark."

Corwin nodded, still in shock. Nia had finally told him the story of all that had happened in Atlantis before she'd come here, and he knew that Ar'an was the creature he'd found on the beach, the one from whom he'd taken Gobaith.

"So. I'm part mermyd." Saying the words out loud somehow made them seem even more absurd. He still couldn't grasp how it could be possible. "Why haven't I felt any longing for the sea, then?" he asked.

Nia shrugged. "You were born and raised on land. You've never known the sea as your home. Why should you long for it? All mermyds have land-dweller ancestors, but we certainly don't long for land."

"Well, isn't . . . don't . . . never mind." He looked down at the sand, trying to order his thoughts. As crazy as it all seemed, some part of him felt a bright hope at the idea that he and Nia shared more than he'd thought. If this were all true, then could the two of them . . . ? "But this still doesn't tell me who, exactly, my father is," he pointed out, pushing away the other thought.

"You may never know," Nia said, sympathy in her

eyes. "I just recently learned that there were wild mermyds, who now and then left Atlantis to swim in the wide sea. The Councils, as well as Ma'el, had spies who informed them of what land-dwellers were up to. Your father might have been any of these."

Corwin kicked the water in frustration. It was annoying to have only half an answer to a question that had haunted him all his life. "So," he said as something else occurred to him. "How did Ma'el know I was part mermyd?"

With his current powers, he is now sensitive to the presence of any oculae, Gobaith informed Corwin. *And you have a partial one.*

"What! I have one of those little throbby lumps?"

Just a bit of one.

"Where?"

In your head. Behind your eyes.

Unable to help himself, Corwin tried to sense its presence, but couldn't.

"That's why you had visions, Corwin," Nia said. "But also why you couldn't control them. It's possible that— well, Ma'el said something to me about experiments he did. That's how I have the oculus, and how Cephan did. Something similar could have happened to you."

"So *that's* why Ma'el wanted me alive along with you!" His heart grew heavy. "And why I've spent my life cursed . . . always bringing people sadness," he went on. "Maybe I should have let Ma'el remove my oculus, as he wanted."

No no no no no no—

"I know, Gobaith, I know." Corwin kept looking at his hands, his skin, his feet, for some clue that any mermyd blood ran in him. He felt very strange, having thought of himself one way for all of his sixteen years and now, just a few moments before, having his entire life turned topsy-turvy. Everything he'd ever done or experienced had to be looked at in a new light. "This is going to take me some time to accept," he said slowly. "Maybe I should hope Ma'el is still alive, so he can tell me more, if he was in fact involved."

"I'd rather not hope that," Nia said, "but he probably is. If so, I'm sure he went back to Atlantis." Again, her face became somber.

Corwin could hold the question from his tongue no longer. "Nia . . . do you . . . do you have any plans? As to when you might . . . go back to the sea . . . for good?" It hurt him to even ask.

Nia gazed back at him and he thought her aquamarine

eyes were lovelier than ever. "I'm afraid it will have to happen soon. It's not that I don't like your land kingdom, Corwin. There are many strange and wondrous things here. But I can't enjoy myself while my people suffer. If any of them are still alive. I am the last Avatar . . . one of the last Avatars," she corrected herself, smiling at him. "It's Gobaith's duty to return as the last Farworlder king, and he's aware of this. He feels ready, although I hope it's not just his youth and spirit that make him so certain. It's also my duty, especially since I . . ." her voice wavered for a moment. "Since I was the one who brought disaster to my people," she finished.

Corwin reached over and took her hand in his. "You couldn't have known that Cephan was lying to you. You couldn't have known that the prophecy your family believed in was wrong."

"But it was *right*," Nia said. "They were just wrong about the *way* in which it would be right."

"Don't try to confuse me with logic," Corwin said, trying to soothe her, even though he knew it was pointless. "It wasn't your fault."

"Even so," Nia said, gazing down at the tide-pool at her feet, "I'm responsible. I must go."

Corwin sighed. "But what can you, or even Gobaith,

do against Ma'el? We only barely defeated him here, on dry land. He'll be much more powerful in the sea, won't he?"

Nia nodded. "Yes, but we can interfere with his power. Just as a small rock in the right place can sink a ship. I might prevent him from doing more harm, at least. And there is another thing. . . ."

"Why is there always another thing?" Corwin asked, rolling his eyes.

Nia splashed him. "Be serious," she said, but she was smiling. "There is one other oculus that Ma'el probably doesn't know about. My father showed me a sword, a ceremonial sword that had been made with an oculus in the hilt. It was to be a gift to the first land-dweller king that might bring peace to the land-dwelling world. But Atlantis hid below the waves before the sword could be given. It was strange, but I could feel the magical power in the sword when others couldn't. I think I know where that sword might be. With its help, we might have enough power to overcome Ma'el, not just interfere."

"I see." Corwin nodded, unsure what else to say. But he could already feel the hole in his heart that would grow large when she left him.

Gobaith slapped his tentacles on the surface of the

water. Corwin sensed that the Farworlder was gently chastising Nia about something.

Suddenly, her eyes opened wide. "Oh, I'm so sorry!" She took his hand in both of hers. "I wasn't listening well to your feelings—you've been worrying that I'd abandon you, but I just thought you were sad at the thought of leaving your homeland."

Corwin blinked, trying to make sense of what she'd said.

"But no, you're wrong," she went on. "Gobaith and I aren't leaving you here, Corwin. You have to come with us. We can't succeed without your power to help us."

"Me? How can I come with you?" Corwin asked in surprise. "Even if it's true that I'm part mermyd, I don't have gills. I can hold my breath for long minutes, but that doesn't mean I can swim all the way down to Atlantis and live there. Even Ma'el said I might drown on the way, and a dry room doesn't sound like a very comfortable place."

Gobaith blew air out of the siphons on either side of his head, making the water bubble. Corwin had come to learn that this was his way of expressing exasperation.

Nia smiled. "Corwin, sometimes I think the unis flows in one of your ears and out the other. Don't you remember the transformation that Ma'el was able to do to himself?

Now that we're strong and well again, Gobaith can help you make these." She fluttered the gills on her neck. "That was how he saved you when you nearly drowned in the castle."

"He . . . he can? He did? I could?" Suddenly the world, and the future, looked very different to Corwin.

Nia laughed. "He can. He did. You could. Will you come with us, Corwin? Will you help me save my people?"

Since meeting you, Corwin thought, *being with you has been the most important thing in my life.*

Nia blushed.

Corwin blushed, too. "Since you know my thoughts, you have to know that I couldn't do anything else."